A FAIR EXCHANGE

Tara Wyndham has a busy life: she manages a beauty salon, That Special Touch, as well as the five-year-old daughter of her ne'er-do-well young brother and single father, Ricky. Things get complicated when Ricky vanishes without a trace, and Tara is apprised of an impending visit from Gray Madison, owner of the business which has recently taken over her salon. And he has a reputation for being utterly ruthless. So why does Tara find herself feeling attracted to him — and what is she to do about Ricky?

Books by Susan Udy
in the Linford Romance Library:

THE CALL OF THE PEACOCK
FORTUNE'S BRIDE
DARK FORTUNE
DANGEROUS LEGACY
REBELLIOUS HEARTS
SUSPICIOUS HEART
TENDER TAKEOVER
DARK SUSPICION
CLIFF HOUSE
THE UNFORGIVING HEART
THE RELUCTANT STAND-IN
I'M WATCHING YOU
FLIGHT OF THE HERON
A TENDER CONFLICT
FRANCESCA
TROUBLE IN PARADISE
THE SHADOW IN THE DARK
SEEING SHADOWS
DARK OBSESSION
DANGEROUS ENCOUNTER
I'LL ALWAYS BE THERE

SUSAN UDY

A FAIR EXCHANGE

Complete and Unabridged

LINFORD
Leicester

First published in Great Britain in 2020

First Linford Edition
published 2020

A catalogue record for this book is available
from the British Library.

ISBN 978–1–4448–4362–0

Published by
F. A. Thorpe (Publishing)
Anstey, Leicestershire

Set by Words & Graphics Ltd.
Anstey, Leicestershire
Printed and bound in Great Britain by
T. J. International Ltd., Padstow, Cornwall

This book is printed on acid-free paper

1

Tara Wyndham glanced at the clock on the kitchen wall. Eight o'clock. Ricky was going to be late for work — again. It was always the same on a Monday. He couldn't get out of bed, or wouldn't get out of bed; she could never decide which. One thing she did know was that she barely saw her brother over the course of any weekend, which invariably meant he'd been spending the majority of his time in one or other of the various clubs or pubs that he frequented with his group of friends before, more often than not, spending the Saturday night elsewhere.

She didn't ask where. On the few occasions that she had, he'd become angry, telling her in no uncertain terms to mind her own business. Events had run true to form this weekend, although he had put in an appearance last evening, albeit briefly. He hadn't mentioned not returning home again, however. She'd tried talking to him several times over the past four or so years, attempting to instil some sense of responsibility in him by pointing out that he now had a five-year-old child to consider; but nothing she said managed to penetrate that immature, and frankly shiftless, attitude of his. She accepted he was only twenty-three and tried to make allowances, but still . . .

Eventually, of course, he'd get the sack, as had happened several times before. There was only so much an employer would tolerate, after all. She walked into the hallway and shouted up the stairs, 'Ricky, it's eight o'clock.' When he didn't respond, she shouted again, even more loudly, 'You're going to be late.'

Still there was no answer. Exasperation took over from mere irritation, and she ran up the stairs to knock on his door.

'Where's Daddy? He's late.'

Tara glanced down at the small girl

standing at the foot of the stairs. Her niece, Daisy, Ricky's daughter, the daughter he seemed to forget he had.

'Yes, and I'm about to find out why,' Tara grimly said as she banged one last time before casting aside any respect for his privacy and pushing the door open.

The room was empty, the bed made. As Ricky never made his bed — that task was left to Tara — it clearly hadn't been slept in. 'God, Ricky,' she muttered, 'what the hell are you playing at? Where are you?' She swept out of the room and descended the stairs.

'Is Daddy still asleep?' Daisy stared up at her from bright blue eyes.

'No.'

'What's he doing, then?'

'He must have left already.' Or, as she'd already surmised, he hadn't returned home at all. 'Did Daddy say anything to you about staying somewhere else last night? At a friend's, maybe?'

Daisy shook her head, her blonde curls bouncing around her heart-shaped face.

Tara didn't recall Ricky taking an overnight bag with him when he'd left the house the previous evening, so he couldn't have been planning to stay somewhere else. He'd have needed some work clothes for today. The garments he'd been wearing last evening wouldn't have been suitable. A stab of anxiety made itself felt at that point. She tried to recall exactly what he'd said as he left the house. He'd told her he had to collect something from someone, and that was all. No mention of not returning home.

She pulled her mobile phone from her handbag and pressed the speed-dial button for her brother's number. But his phone was either switched off or he was in a dead zone, because all she heard was an electronic message saying 'the number you have called is currently unavailable'. She had to be content with leaving a message, asking him to call her, and hope he'd eventually get in touch.

'Auntie Tara.' Daisy was by this time

looking as anxious as Tara felt. For a five-year-old, she was remarkably perceptive.

'It's okay, darling. He's obviously busy. I'll try him later. Now, it's time for you to get ready for school.'

⋆　⋆　⋆

Once she'd dropped her niece at school, Tara drove to the beauty salon that she managed: That Special Touch. It was one of a nationwide chain and offered aromatherapy massages, facials and nail treatments for both hands and feet. The other members of staff weren't in yet, so Tara's first task was to try Ricky's number again. And again, she got the same response. His phone must definitely be turned off.

'For God's sake, Ricky,' she muttered, 'where the hell are you?'

She sighed.

The trouble with Ricky was he was simply too irresponsible, too feckless to be a father. He'd only been eighteen when Daisy was born, and an immature eighteen at that. The mother, who'd been a mere sixteen, had decided, upon being handed the crying, wriggling baby as she was discharged from the hospital, that she wouldn't be able to cope, and two days later had arrived at Ricky and Tara's door, saying he'd have to take care of her. She'd handed Daisy to him and disappeared. That had been the last either of them had seen of her.

Tara had taken one look at the tiny scrap of humanity, who after all hadn't asked to be born, and said, 'I'll help you, Ricky. Don't worry. We'll care for her together.'

However, she hadn't anticipated being the main carer, because the truth was Ricky didn't seem to want to know his daughter. He much preferred being out with his mates to staying at home and looking after Daisy. Tara had hoped this would change the older he became; but sadly, it hadn't. He still left the bulk of the care of the small girl to his sister.

The end result of this was that Tara's

social life had more or less vanished. She didn't know what she would have done without the help of her friend, Lizzie, who cared for Daisy while Tara worked. The same friend who now met Daisy from school five days a week and also had charge of her all day on a Saturday. Once Tara had finished work for the day, she then collected her and brought her home.

Lizzie had her own daughter, Gemma, who was the same age as Daisy, and they had become staunch friends. But the main thing was that Lizzie loved Daisy as if she were her own. So much so, that she had initially refused any payment for the childminding. Tara, however, had insisted, although it had been a bit of a struggle to manage financially to start with. But as Tara's circumstances improved — she'd been promoted to the position of manager of the salon a couple of years ago — things became easier. And Ricky did contribute financially now and again, but only now and again. The main burden of their living expenses fell squarely upon Tara.

Add to that the fact that Tara had also brought up Ricky in the aftermath of their parents' deaths in a motorway pile-up nine years ago, and she hadn't been as intimidated at the responsibility of caring for a baby as she might have been. Fortunately, she'd been twenty-one at the time of her parents' death, so social services had deemed her mature enough to have the total care of a fourteen-year-old boy. It hadn't been easy, even so. Ricky had been head-strong even then, and that hadn't changed — as was demonstrated by the fact that Tara didn't at present know his whereabouts.

As if this wasn't enough, to add to her woes, she'd heard a worrying piece of news. Several other branches of That Special Touch had been closed down, mainly in the north of the country; but even so, it gave Tara considerable cause for concern. In fact, she'd begun to consider trying to raise a mortgage in order to buy the salon.

Another company had taken over the chain six months ago: Madison International. This was owned by someone called Gray Madison, a very wealthy and influential businessman she'd heard, with various companies all over the country. And, by all accounts, utterly ruthless. Tara had never met him and didn't expect to. She simply couldn't imagine him turning up at Mallow End, the small but picturesque town in the Midlands, a few miles from Worcester, in which the salon was situated and where Tara lived. Luckily, it was still profitable — just; although they had taken a bit more of a hit over the past three or four months, despite some women still travelling from a five- or six-mile radius for their treatments. Tara was sure, given a free hand, that she could improve the turnover and thus increase her client list.

The doorbell chimed as other members of staff came in. There were five in all, including Tara. Lucy and Mandy provided the various nail treatments, although it was Lucy's day off today.

Annie and Sara were the aromatherapists. Tara had made sure she was skilled in each of the procedures, so that she could help out wherever she was needed; for example when they were particularly busy, which had been most of the time up until four months ago. Since then, things had slowed down; disturbingly so.

The postman followed them in and handed Tara several items of mail. She flicked through the envelopes as she greeted her co-workers. There was one white envelope amongst the brown. It was addressed to her personally, rather than the salon's name. She slid a finger under the seal and opened it. She pulled out the single sheet of paper. Her glance flicked to the name at the bottom. Gray Madison, Company Director.

She frowned. What was this? Her heart gave an almighty lurch. The warning that they were about to be closed down? She hadn't expected a letter. Most things were communicated by text or email nowadays. Clearly Gray Madison was a member of the old school. A man of mature years, no doubt.

She strode into the room at the back of the salon that served both as an office and staff room. There were two other rooms alongside, both treatment rooms for massages and facials. The nails were done in the main body of the salon. Tara began to read:

Dear Ms Wyndham,

I am going to be personally visiting each and every Special Touch salon in the next few weeks with a view to the streamlining of the chain as a whole. In today's difficult business climate, we need to ensure that each salon is operating at the highest levels of efficiency and profitability.

I should be getting to you shortly. I look forward to meeting you to discuss turnover and, as a result of those figures, plans for the future.

Yours sincerely,
Gray Madison.

Tara tossed the letter onto her desk. Just as she'd feared, he was planning to close them down. Clearly, if you weren't making bucket loads of money for him, you were out. Which indicated he was more than living up to his reputation of ruthlessness. Well, she'd see about that. In fact, she was prepared to fight him every step of the way if it came to it. Even if that entailed somehow finding the means to buy the salon from him.

One point in her favour was the fact that she had no existing mortgage. The house she and Ricky lived in, a three-bedroom semi, had been left them by her parents. A life insurance policy taken out by her father had taken care of whatever had been owing on it. As well as that, there had been a fairly substantial amount of money. Edward Wyndham had been a prudent man, and a portion of his salary had been regularly and carefully invested over the years. By no means could it have been described as a fortune, but it had made life considerably easier for her and Ricky for a while.

'Hey, what's bothering you? You're looking a bit down.'

Tara held out the letter to Annie, her main confidante and chief assistant. Although Annie obviously knew their profits were dipping, Tara hadn't confided the true extent of the reduction. With Dave, Annie's husband, out of work, she hadn't wanted to worry her, maybe unnecessarily, and she'd kept hoping the current financial problems would prove no more than a blip and things would start to pick up again. As that had failed to materialise, Tara felt she should be honest with her, especially in the light of Gray Madison preparing to visit. She knew she could rely on Annie to keep her mouth zipped. She didn't want the other staff members to know their jobs could be in jeopardy in case they decided to find new positions and leave. That would be a catastrophe; the death knell to the salon, even. They were all fully trained and would be hard, if not impossible, to replace.

'Oh, good grief,' Annie murmured. 'Does this mean closure? Could I lose my job too? Because I've heard a few rumours about this guy. He doesn't suffer fools or loss-makers gladly.'

Tara shrugged. 'I'm no wiser than you. But let's not think the worst.'

'Oh well, we'll just have to wait and see.' She eyed Tara then. 'I'm sure we'll be okay. We make a fairly respectable profit, don't we? I know we've been quieter lately.'

'Well, we don't make as much profit as we used to, so . . . ' Once more, Tara shrugged.

'Oh God,' Annie moaned. 'You should have told me. What can we do?'

'Well, let's not panic for a start. We're fairly well-booked this week.'

'I'll ring round the clients who haven't made appointments and get them in. If he's going to be dropping in on us, we need to at least look busy.'

'You can try, but if they don't need

— or want — treatments, there's not a lot we can do.'

'We could offer them a discount.'

'Wouldn't that rather defeat the purpose? And I really need the approval of head office for that.'

'Hmmm. Yeah. Okay, leave it with me. I've got a lull between appointments this afternoon. I'll try a few of my clients to start with.'

'No discounts though, Annie,' Tara warned.

The truth was, though, if anyone could get more clients in, it was Annie. With her cheerful disposition and readiness to listen to their problems, she was the most popular member of staff by far. Clients requested her by name. But Mondays were always quiet days. If it had been up to Tara, she'd have closed the salon that day and saved on overheads. But it was company policy to open six days a week. Staff members had a day off each during the week, hence Lucy's absence today. Tara, of course, worked the full six days. It wasn't mandatory; it was her choice.

Oh well, let the day begin.

Tara went to the mirror on the office wall to check that she looked neat and tidy. She sighed. Her hazel eyes looked visibly troubled. She needed to buck herself and her mood up. She didn't want the clients wondering what was wrong. At least her hair was tidy. It hung, the colour of a horse chestnut, thickly and completely straight to a fraction above her shoulders, with no hint of a wave or a curl. It drove her crazy, appearing, in her opinion, lacklustre and lank, even though her friends always told her how much they envied its silky smoothness. She pulled some lipstick from her handbag and reapplied it to her full lips, then dabbed a hint of blusher onto her paler-than-usual high-boned cheeks.

She then turned her attention to her clothes, tucking her blouse back into the waist of her skirt before smoothing her hands over the curve of her hips.

She gave another even more heartfelt sigh then. Breasts that she considered too large filled her blouse to capacity. In fact, a couple of the buttons looked under distinct strain. She'd have to lose weight; it wasn't a good look to have buttons on the point of popping off. Her only reasonable features, again in her opinion, were her legs, with their shapely calves and neat ankles. And she was modestly proud of those.

However, she hadn't got time to worry about how she looked. And well, that was the least of her problems.

She followed Annie into the salon. She had a few appointments of her own today with Lucy being absent, so any managerial tasks, like bringing the accounts up to date, would have to wait. And maybe, if she kept busy, she'd even manage to put her worries to one side. There was nothing she could do until she'd seen Gray Madison and learnt what it was he intended for them.

★ ★ ★

The day passed relatively quickly, with a few walk-ins wanting their nails done. One asked for a facial as well. These were extra to the appointments, so that cheered Tara somewhat. It all added to their turnover figure.

She did find time to try Ricky's number again, but as had happened previously, he wasn't taking calls. Her anxiety deepened, even though this wasn't the first time he'd done a disappearing act. He seemed to think he could come and go as he pleased, and no one should complain, least of all her. But the truth was that he'd lost countless jobs because of his irresponsible attitude and behaviour. His current work was stacking shelves in a DIY centre. 'Boring as hell.' he'd told her. 'I'm on the lookout for something better.'

Could he have found it and just left, both present job and home? It seemed unlikely. He had no particular talent for anything, drifting aimlessly from one job to another. Tara doubted he'd be able to support himself, even with a new job. In fact, without her income, they'd have been practically on the breadline more than once. The money her father had left them had been used up several years ago.

But aside from all of this, her chief worry was what he was up to. She prayed it wasn't anything illegal, or that he wasn't in some sort of trouble. She had no idea of the sort of people he currently mixed with. All she did know was that, for the past few weeks, he'd been flashing quite a bit more money around, which, with no obvious source or explanation, was deeply troubling. When she'd asked him where he was getting it from, he'd simply brushed her concern away.

'I've got it,' he'd said, 'so stop worrying. It's none of your business where it's come from, anyway.'

She'd wondered at one point if he was gambling. But whatever he was doing, she certainly saw none of the cash. Which meant he must be spending it on something, because Ricky had never been a saver. Maybe she should ring the police and report him missing? She chewed at her bottom lip. That did seem a bit extreme. It had only been a few hours since she'd seen him, after all. In which case, it was unlikely the police would do anything about it. And what if he was involved in some sort of criminal activity? Did she really want them investigating him?

Ricky had certainly changed over the past few months, becoming even moodier than usual and highly unpredictable. When she'd tentatively asked him if everything was okay, he'd simply snapped at her and told her yet again to mind her own business. In fact, he was increasingly only polite when he wanted something. And, more disturbingly, he was showing even less interest in Daisy than normal. Tara had hoped that as the little girl grew older, he'd become more of a father to her. That hadn't happened, and didn't seem likely to any time soon.

However, by the time she closed the salon that afternoon, she felt a little more cheerful. They'd had a pleasingly busy day, which meant she still hadn't got round to updating the accounts. She needed to get down to it. Gray Madison, whenever he showed up, would doubtless demand to see her figures for the previous month. He would, in all likelihood, know them up until then. It was all on computer nowadays, after all. So the recent drop in turnover was almost certainly the prime factor behind his planned visit.

She collected Daisy on her way back from Lizzie's, and they were in the house by six thirty.

'Is Daddy home?' Daisy asked the minute they were inside.

'Well, his car's not outside so . . . '

A few months ago, before his sudden show of wealth, Ricky had managed to get himself an old car. 'It's going cheap because it's a mate selling it. He's letting me have it for five hundred quid.' Which Tara had loaned him,

21

naturally, and which, despite his inex-
plicable increase in income, he hadn't
as yet repaid.

Daisy's small face fell. 'I want to see
him. I need to tell him about Melanie.'

Tara glanced down at her niece.
'What about Melanie?' Melanie had
recently become her best friend.

'She pushed me and I nearly fell
down.'

'Why did she do that?'

'She said she doesn't like me
anymore.' Daisy's bottom lip quivered
as her eyes filled with tears.

Tara crouched down so that her head
was on a level with Daisy's. 'I'm sure
she doesn't mean it.'

She hugged her niece before standing
up once more to walk further into the
house, Daisy at her side. Tara's brief
glance around revealed no sign that
Ricky had been there.

'She does!' Daisy shouted as she ran
up the stairs to her bedroom.

'Daisy — ?'

But it was no use. The little girl

disappeared into her room and slammed the door behind her. Tara sighed. As if she didn't have enough to worry about, what with Ricky's disappearance and the unpredictable future of the salon.

For the bitter truth was she could pretty soon find herself out of a job — and then what would they all do?

2

By the following morning, and with still no word from her brother, Tara was becoming seriously worried. She'd tried phoning him repeatedly last evening and then again this morning, with the same result. His phone was evidently still turned off. Why would he do that? Unless — could he have lost it? But surely he'd have let her know that somehow; borrowed a phone. As indifferent to her and Daisy as he was nowadays, he must know she'd worry.

Daisy, not surprisingly, had picked up on her aunt's anxiety; and that, combined with her friend's treatment the previous day, resulted in her becoming fretful and tearful.

'I need to see my daddy. Where is he?'

'I don't know, darling. He's probably busy.'

'No,' the little girl shouted, 'he's not. He's gone away — he's left me.' She began to cry, noisily and heartbreakingly.

Tara lifted her onto her knee and held her close. 'He won't have left you,' she quietly reassured the little girl. 'He'll be back, you'll see.'

But Daisy wouldn't be consoled, although eventually her sobs did lessen and finally stop.

'Come on, sweetie, it's time to go. You can't be late for school.'

'No,' the small girl cried. 'I don't want to go.' Her bottom lip protruded and she crossed her arms across her chest as if to emphasize her refusal.

'Of course you do. You love school.'

'Don't.' Her lip protruded even further.

'Daisy — please. I have a lot of work to do.' Tara had planned to spend the first couple of hours updating her computer accounts She had to have them ready for Gray Madison's inspection, and didn't want to provide him with any sort of reason — excuse — to close the salon. There were five jobs at stake. 'What will your teacher think if you don't turn up?'

'Don't care.'

'Well, I do. So come on, coat on. The warm one.' It was a chilly and wet early March morning.

Finally, she managed to persuade Daisy to do as she asked, and they left the house. Daisy, determined to show she wasn't completely beaten, sat in the rear of the car, muttering all the way until Tara's patience in the end evaporated. 'Be quiet — what will your teacher say if you arrive in such a bad mood?'

The arms crossed once again as she muttered, 'Don't care.'

However, when they pulled up at the school gate and Daisy spotted her friend, Melanie, obviously waiting for her, her mood instantly lightened and she eagerly climbed from the car and ran towards her.

Tara breathed a huge sigh of relief.

Now she could continue to work without having to worry about her niece. She drove off, waving to the two girls, who were walking into the playground arm in arm, talking all the while with a great deal of animation. With luck, she'd have a good hour or two to catch up on her computer work. She had no appointments; all four assistants were working today.

However, things didn't work out that way. She did manage to make a start, but then several women phoned on the off chance that they could have the treatment they wanted that day. Unwilling to turn any business down, and as the four therapists were booked all day, Tara herself carried out the treatments. Every little bit would help their financial situation. And if things kept going this way — well, Gray Madison would have no reason to close them down.

It was almost lunchtime before she finished and retreated to the small back room for a short break. However, that wasn't to be, as she heard the shop door opening. A walk-in client? Was she ever going to have the time to complete her computer work? She walked back into the main salon, automatically tidying up as she went. She heard a man's voice asking, 'Tara Wyndham?' and she looked up, already smiling a welcome, to be confronted by a tall, good-looking man with piercing amber eyes standing by the side of Annie. Wow! Her breath caught in her throat. He must be at least six foot one or two. He towered above Annie. What on earth could he want? She couldn't imagine he required any sort of treatment at all. He was well-nigh perfect.

She smothered a sigh of longing and said, 'That's me. How can I help you?'

'Good afternoon. I'm Gray Madison. You should have had a letter from me concerning this visit.'

'Oh.' Once again, Tara's breath caught. This wasn't the member of the old school that she'd been expecting. Far from it. He couldn't be more than mid-thirties. Which was maybe why he hadn't had the courtesy to make a proper appointment? 'Well, yes, I-I wasn't expecting — '

'You weren't expecting me? What did you think my letter meant?' A single eyebrow was raised at her; a critical eyebrow, she decided. An arrogant eyebrow, even.

'I — um, I wasn't expecting you so soon.' God, how lame did she sound?

'Well, here I am.' He held out an immaculately cared-for hand for her to take.

Which was extremely disconcerting, as her arms and hands were full of the bottles, jars, pots, used cloths, and towels that she'd gathered up on her way, which of course meant she couldn't respond to the gesture. She felt at an immediate disadvantage, and eyed him. Could that be what he intended? There was certainly a strange glint to his eye which bore out her suspicion. He intended to have the upper hand right from the start. Sneaky. It also didn't bode well for the future of the salon. If he was intent on closing them down, what chance did she have to persuade him otherwise? Okay, their turnover was up, but was it up sufficiently to stop him doing what he wanted to?

She walked towards a side table and deposited her load upon it. She then swivelled back to face him, not offering her own hand in return. It was a small gesture, but one that indicated that she was irritated at the way he'd descended upon them. She saw a flicker in his eye as he registered the slight, but he made no comment. She felt a spurt of triumph.

'I thought you might have set a day and time for your visit. That way I could have been prepared for you.'

'Quite so. That's not my way of working, however.'

No, she mused. Catching people off balance. That was much more his way. Well, he'd succeeded in his intention and caught her completely unprepared.

'You don't employ anyone to tidy up after you all, then?' He glanced around the salon, clearly searching for something else to criticize.

'No, we find it more cost-effective to do it ourselves.'

His one eyebrow lifted again. It was obviously a favourite tactic of his. Again, one that could intimidate and overawe, thus making sure he got his own way. Well, it wasn't going to work with her. She'd make sure of that.

'Isn't that rather a waste of time that could be spent on your clients' needs?' The words were softly spoken, but for all that were an unmistakable criticism. 'It's why I like to choose my own time to visit, to see the way that people work. It provides a more accurate way of assessing the business as well as the efficiency and skill of the staff.'

Tara decided to ignore that.

'Is there somewhere more private that we can talk?' He'd obviously become aware of the interest being shown by the four therapists as well as the clients that were still there.

'Yes, of course.' She turned and led

the way into the small back room — which she hadn't bothered to tidy up. She'd planned to do it after they'd all had their lunches. She nibbled at her lower lip as she gazed around. Dammit. There were several dirty coffee cups; a half-empty cafetiere; the remains of a packet of biscuits, crumbs and all; spilt coffee; sugar granules where someone had missed their cup and hadn't bothered clearing them up. Once again, his narrowed gaze swept over it all. This time, though, he made no comment. He didn't need to. His expression said it all for him. It was one of resigned disdain.

'Please,' Tara said, indicating a chair, 'sit down. Can I offer you some coffee?' Hastily, she swept some crumbs off the seat.

'Thank you — no.' He didn't actually turn his nose up, but he might as well have done. Probably afraid he'd catch something.

Thoroughly irritated now, Tara bit out, 'Well, if you don't mind, I'll have one. It's my first chance in three hours.'

He sat down rather tentatively, and only after a keen glance at the seat first. He couldn't have made his feelings plainer. *What a dump*, he was obviously thinking.

Tara's heart plummeted along with her spirit. He intended to close them down. If he hadn't decided before he'd arrived, he most likely had now.

'So how are you finding things?' he asked out of the blue.

She stared at him, eyes wide, visibly thrown by his question. 'Uh — well — I know, more or less, where everything is.' She glanced around the small room. 'I know it's a bit untidy.'

'No.' He grinned then, properly grinned at her, and the features that had been relatively handsome were transformed into mind-blowing good looks. Looks fit for the cinema screen, in fact.

She gave a small gasp, her eyes widening again at him, as her lips parted.

'I mean — how are you finding business?'

'Haven't you seen the figures for the last six months? Well, up until last month? I haven't quite completed February's yet.' Hah! Not quite completed them? She'd barely started them. She wasn't about to admit that to him, though. She had no intention of providing him with yet another reason to display his scornful disapproval.

'Yes, of course, but I like to get the manager's perspective on things as a whole. Figures can tell you a lot, but I rely more on the personal viewpoint — what the intentions are for the future, the growth plans, motivations, ambition, that sort of thing.'

She studied him more closely now. His hair was thick, not too long, and a dark blond. His nose, she supposed, could be described as Grecian. His jawline was chiselled, and his cheek-bones were high and razor-sharp. As for his mouth — well, that had a distinctly sensual look to the full bottom lip. He'd be great to kiss . . .

Belatedly, and as an unexpected glint lit his amber eyes, she realised he'd been only too aware of her keen examination, and most likely her thoughts as well. Her mother always said she could read her like an open book. Clearly, nothing had changed in that respect. She felt her cheeks warming as she became aware of the manner in which his gaze was now lingering on her, on her face, her eyes, her hair, the pulse that throbbed in the base of her throat, and finally on the full breasts that she suspected were clearly outlined beneath the thin three-quarter-length overall that she wore when administering treatments. For the third time, she felt the breath catching in her throat and she glanced down, only to see that not only the shape of her breasts was fully visible, but that her skirt had also ridden up, exposing several inches of shapely thigh, and making it look as if she was wearing practically nothing beneath the overall. She swiftly tugged it back down, not daring to look at him to see what he was making of it all.

'So,' he murmured throatily, 'again — how are you finding things? I noticed from your most recent figures that profits are down.' He regarded her, his gaze a penetrating one. It was as if he could see straight through her — and her clothes.

Tara cleared her throat in an attempt to defuse the tension that had sprung up between them — sexual tension, unless she was mistaken about the look in his eye. 'Um — well, as you say our profits have fallen slightly, but we are still profitable. We've been getting a lot of walk-in clients rather than fixed appointments.'

'I see.' His gaze narrowed at her. 'From the state of the salon, you're clearly busy, but I would prefer to see it kept a little more tidy. Having said that, it does give the appearance of a fully occupied and busy team.' He shrugged, drawing her gaze to the breadth of his shoulders beneath the perfectly tailored jacket. 'We'll see how it goes over the next three months, but I do expect to see a distinct increase in your profits, so give some thought about how to achieve that.' He paused then, his narrowed gaze still fixed upon her, making both her breath and her pulse quicken. 'I'm having a drinks party at my home — Osborne House, at Abbotsleigh. Do you know it?'

'I don't think so. I know of Abbotsleigh, of course, but I've not been there,' she hastened to add.

'Well . . . ' He pulled a card from his top jacket pocket. ' . . . here's the address and my phone numbers, mobile and landline at home. I'd like you to come. I'm inviting some of the other managers. A mixed bag, but a couple of them run salons like yours, so you might find it helpful to learn how they operate in order to increase their profit margins.'

She regarded the card. Abbotsleigh was a village seven or eight miles from

Mallow End. She'd passed through it a couple of times on her way somewhere else, but hadn't stopped. There wasn't much there; a couple of small shops and a pub, if she remembered correctly. In fact, she would have described it as a hamlet if asked, rather than a village. It was charmingly picturesque with a river winding through it, a pretty stone footbridge across it, and roads that were lined with beeches and horse chestnuts. As for Osborne House, she thought she knew where it was; she might even have passed it. What houses there were there — and there hadn't been many — were all very substantial properties. Abbotsleigh was obviously the stomping ground for the rich. No cheaper, affordable housing there.

'I've not long moved in, four or five months ago. I'd been finding the southeast increasingly unpleasant to live in; so much congestion everywhere. I'm a country soul at heart. In fact, I was born not far from here. Compton Cross. Do you know it?'

'I know it, yes.' That too was not much more than a hamlet a couple of miles from Abbotsleigh. It was also largely inhabited by wealthy people, judging by the size of the houses. An enclave, in other words, of the rich and privileged.

'So will you come?' That infernal eyebrow once again rose. 'A week tomorrow, Wednesday, at 7 o'clock.'

Tara could hardly say no, as much as she was tempted to. He'd made it sound like an invitation, but she was pretty sure he wouldn't be pleased if she declined, and it was obviously prudent not to ruffle his feathers just now.

'Yes, I'd like that,' she replied. 'Thank you.'

'I'm confident that you'll find it interesting and helpful, even. It's always good to exchange views with your contemporaries, don't you find?'

'Quite — yes.' Her heart pounded in her chest as she nervously wondered what she was letting herself in for.

She'd have to ask Lizzie to babysit, but she was sure she would. She'd done it before — well, a couple of times. It wasn't a regular occurrence, because Tara no longer went out in the evenings. Mainly because after a day in the salon she was too tired, and it would be no good relying on Ricky, even if he was at home. Her anxiety kicked back in as she thought of her brother. Maybe he'd be there when she got home. God, she hoped so.

'Right then.' Gray Madison got to his feet. 'I'll see you at the party. Till then.' He held out his hand, and this time hers were free to take it. He had a firm clasp as his long fingers wrapped themselves around hers, almost in a caress. 'Goodbye.'

Tara also stood up. 'I-I'll show you out.'

'No need. I'm sure I'll find the way.' And he flashed that stunning grin once more.

Tara felt the breath leave her body in a discernible gasp. With those looks and the fortune he'd apparently accumulated, he must have women queuing up for him. He strode through the salon, smiling at the clients who remained there as he went. As for the girls who were tending to them, they looked gobsmacked.

Once he'd closed the door behind him, Annie softly said, 'Wow! And double wow! Who'd have thought he'd look like that?'

'I know,' Tara replied. 'I'd had him down as years older.'

'Yeah, and me. Did you see his car?' Annie went on.

'It was only a flippin' Ferrari,' Lucy eagerly put in.

Even as she spoke, the deep-throated roar of a powerful engine reached them.

'That's him,' Annie giggled.

At this, her client spoke up. 'Who was that?'

'My boss,' Tara told her. 'Gray Madison. He owns this salon and many others besides.'

'Gray Madison. Yeah, I've heard all about him. Made millions in just a few years. A bit of a tyrant, though, so you'd all better watch yourselves. If he's dissatisfied with you for any reason, you're out. He closed down the engineering firm that my brother worked for a couple of months ago. Couldn't envisage a future for it, so they all lost their jobs, and he couldn't have cared less. I've also heard he's a terrible womaniser, so be warned, ladies.'

Tara felt a sharp stab of misgiving. Not only was he a ruthless hatchet man, he was a womaniser to boot. What chance did she have against someone like that? She had to increase their profitability; she had to. And that meant either raising prices, which she was loath to do, even if she obtained company approval, or bringing in more clients and soon. It seemed an impossible feat, and certainly not one achievable in a matter of a few days. But she had to try.

★ ★ ★

Never one to give up easily, that same evening Tara stayed late at the salon after the other women had gone, designing and then printing off leaflets advertising the services they offered. They'd be ready to post locally to begin with, and if that produced satisfactory results like an increase in their client list, then she'd extend it to other areas. There'd be a cost, naturally — postage, for one thing — but if they acquired more clients, it would excuse the extra expenditure. And, hopefully, it would demonstrate the initiative and drive that Gray apparently wanted to see.

By the time she got to Lizzie's, it was almost seven o'clock.

'Thank you so much, Lizzie.'

'That's okay. I'm always willing to keep her a bit longer, you know that. She's had her tea with Gemma.'

Daisy ran to Tara. 'Is Daddy home?'

Tara felt rather than saw the concern in Lizzie's expression. 'She says Ricky hasn't been home for a day or two. Is he okay?'

43

Tara rolled her eyes. 'Who knows? He'll be back when he's ready.' She lowered her voice to a murmur. 'I just wish he'd ring me.'

'He will, I'm sure. He must know how Daisy worries.'

'I'm sure he does. I'm just not so sure he cares.'

She refused Lizzie's offer of a cup of tea. 'I'd better get this imp home and to bed. School again tomorrow.' She secured Daisy into her car seat in the rear and drove swiftly home. There was still no sign of Ricky's car, either on the driveway or at the kerbside. She sighed softly, not wanting Daisy to hear. Maybe he'd been back and had left her a note?

Daisy freed herself of the restraining strap and leapt from the car, running to the front door, crying, 'Daddy, Daddy,' through the letterbox.

Tara followed more slowly, praying there'd be some sign that Ricky had been back. She opened the door, and Daisy slid past her to run inside.

'Daddy, I'm back.'

As Tara had feared, there was no response. She tightened her lips as anger suffused her. How could Ricky do this? To Daisy? To her? How could he be so cruel? He must know how much Daisy loved him.

Daisy ran through each room. Ricky wasn't there. She began to cry. 'I want my Daddy.'

Tara sat down on the settee and cuddled the child against her. 'I know you do, sweetheart, but he'll be back. He's probably had some important business to attend to.'

But as she spoke, all she could think was, maybe it was time to ring the police. Ricky had been gone for a couple of days, which wasn't all that long, but — with no word at all? She told herself it wasn't the first time he'd done this — although admittedly, he hadn't for a while now. But somehow, on this occasion, it didn't help. With Daisy older and justifiably distressed by his unexplained absence, she felt she should take some sort of action. And, in truth, it did feel different this time for some reason. What if something had happened to him? An accident, maybe? Though she would surely have heard if that was the case.

She'd get Daisy up to bed, and then she'd decide on the best way forward. Although what the police could do, she didn't know. Her brother was a grown man, and grown men disappeared of their own volition all the time. Still, at least she would have reported it.

3

With Daisy tucked beneath her duvet along with her teddy bear, and her favourite story read twice, Tara returned downstairs. She'd made her decision: she'd ring the police. She picked up the phone and tapped out the number 999.

As she'd anticipated, they were no help at all.

'He's a grown man,' the call handler, a woman, told her, 'and he's only been gone a short while. With no evidence of any harm having come to him — etc, etc.' Finally, she suggested, 'You could ring round the local hospitals.'

Which Tara did. With no luck there, either.

At that point, she was at a loss as to what to do next. She'd already checked the contents of his wardrobe and drawers, and, as far as she could tell, there was nothing missing; certainly no worrying spaces. Everything seemed to be there, apart from what he'd been wearing, of course. Which in itself was disturbing, because she regarded it as an indication that he hadn't been prepared to remain away from home; at least, not for more than a day or so.

She'd have to be patient and wait, and trust he'd return soon — for Daisy's sake if nothing else. It had only been two days, after all.

She prepared herself some supper, scrambled eggs on toast, and sat in front of the TV to eat it. But even a repeat episode of one of her favourite series, *Shetland*, failed to dislodge her worries over her brother's absence. So when the landline rang at ten o'clock, sure that it would be Ricky, she rushed to pick it up. Although why he'd ring on that and not her mobile, she didn't know.

However, it wasn't Ricky's voice that came down the line; it was a stranger's. 'I want to speak to Ricky.'

'I'm afraid he's not here. I'm not sure

where he is at the moment. I've been expecting a call.'

The gravelly voice cut her words off. 'I've tried his mobile and he's not answering. I need to speak to him — urgently.'

You and me both, Tara reflected. 'Yes, I've had the same response.'

'Really?' The tone of his voice now was one of extreme scepticism. Of accusation, even. 'You don't know where he is? Are you sure about that?'

'Of course I'm sure.' His tone was beginning to irritate her. Did he think she was lying? Apparently so, she decided. Determined to remain calm in the face of his rudeness, she politely asked, 'If you tell me your name, I'll — '

'Never you mind what my name is. You tell him — when you do speak to him, that is — that he has something of mine and I want it back. He'll know who I am. You tell him if he doesn't deliver, I'll take something of his. Something he won't want to lose.

That'll be a fair exchange, wouldn't you say?'

'Well, I — ' But, whoever it had been, he'd hung up.

Tara frowned as she replaced the receiver onto its base. What on earth was all that about? Ricky had something of his? What? Dear God, had Ricky stolen something? Could that be why he'd disappeared? Could he be on the run?

If that was what had indeed happened, Tara could hardly ring the police again and tell them about the mysterious caller and his accusation. It could be the trigger for an investigation, and well, that could land Ricky in real trouble. In jail, even. Could it be true, that her brother was a thief? What should she do?

For the first time in years, she longed to be able to speak to her father. He'd have known how to handle a situation like this. First of all, though, she needed to speak again to the man who'd called, to try and find out what had happened exactly. What it was that Ricky had taken. She dialled 1471 to obtain his number, but as she should have expected, it had been withheld. She slammed the receiver down. What now?

But more importantly at the moment was, what the hell was she to tell Daisy?

* * *

Daisy awoke the next morning and set about asking questions which Tara had no idea how to answer.

'Has Daddy phoned you?'

'No, he hasn't. But he will, I'm sure.' Somehow, and she didn't know how, she managed to sound convincing. 'He'll know we're worried about him.'

The second she'd said this, she knew she'd made a mistake. Daisy's glance sharpened. At certain times — like now — the little girl could sound many years older than the five that she was. 'You're worried? What's happened to him?'

'Nothing, darling, I'm sure of that.' Oh, if only that were true.

But evidently Daisy accepted this because her next question was, 'Have you washed my shorts and T-shirt? Because I've got PE this morning.'

Luckily, Tara had remembered them the evening before, so, breathing a sigh of relief at her escape from having to try and answer any more questions about Ricky, she hurried to fetch them from the clothes basket.

'You haven't ironed them,' Daisy wailed. 'I'll look a complete mess.' Tears sprang into her eyes. She had a thing about creased clothes.

'No, wait. Look, I'll smooth them out.' And Tara did, using both hands. 'There, good as new.'

'No, they're not.' However, Daisy took them and pushed them into her gym bag before they finally left the house and headed for school, with Daisy grumbling non-stop the entire way.

★ ★ ★

To Tara's relief, it was another reassuringly busy day at the salon; and as such, it would be pushing their profits up, so maybe this month's figures weren't going to be as bad as she'd feared.

She did manage to grab some lunch, even when her closest friend, Bel, popped in to see her. Bel worked at a nearby solicitor's office just a few buildings along from the salon.

'Hey, who was the guy I saw leaving here yesterday and climbing into a Ferrari?'

Tara rolled her eyes, at the same time taking a last bite of her sandwich. Curiosity should have been Bel's middle name, rather than the more mundane Elizabeth — her mother's name — that it was. There wasn't much going on in Mallow End that she missed. Bel could be relied on to be on top of all the latest and juiciest gossip. Not that Tara really approved of gossip; even so, she wasn't averse to listening to the odd snippet.

'Do you spend all day at the office window?'

'No.' Bel sounded indignant. 'I just happened to have stopped for lunch and was looking out. So, who was it? He couldn't have been there for a facial. He didn't look the type. Mind you, there wouldn't be much you could do to improve his looks, in any case. 'Gorgeous' was the description that sprang to mind. 'Bloody gorgeous', in fact.'

'Mmm.'

'Is that all you can say? Mmm? So.' Bel's expression was one of impatient anticipation now. 'Come on, give — all the details.'

'He's Gray Madison.'

Bel looked bewildered.

'I told you. My boss? The man who took over the chain — six months ago.'

'Oh, yes, of course you did. Wow!'

Was that all the women she knew could say? Tara mused. Wow!

'What wouldn't I give for a boss who looked like that — instead of the withered old stick that I work for. And he's driving a bloody Ferrari, to boot. A

54

chick magnet if ever I saw one.'

'I'm sure.' Tara's tone was a tart one now. Really, was she the only woman to see the real nature of the man? Mind you, in all fairness, she'd been the only one to actually talk to him and to have the opportunity to glimpse the — well, unabashed sensuality within his look. 'But then, I've been reliably informed that he's a terrible womaniser.'

'I'll take my chances,' and Bel gave a vulgar snort. 'So-o, what was he doing in sleepy Mallow End?'

'Checking up on me,' Tara drily retorted.

'Really? What have you been doing to make a hunk like that come looking for you?'

'I'm not making sufficient money for him — at a guess.'

'Ah. So — ?' Bel raised both eyebrows. 'What does that mean?'

'The closure of the salon if I don't increase turnover and profits, I would imagine. He's got the reputation of being a tad ruthless — so I've heard.'

'Oh dear. You'll just have to seduce him, then — not too arduous a task, I wouldn't think. And certainly not out of the question.' Bel raised her eyebrows. 'With a figure like yours, you should have no trouble.'

Tara ignored all of that. Such bluntness was typical of her friend, and she'd learnt over the years to ignore her. So instead of retaliating, she said, 'He's asked me to a drinks party he's giving for some of his employees — next Wednesday at his home, Osborne House.'

'Where's that then?'

'Abbotsleigh.'

Bel's eyes had widened into saucers. 'Oh, I think I know it — My God, he must have shedloads of money then, because I heard it went for somewhere in the region of two million pounds. Mind you, it had been on the market for several months, so he might have got it for a bit less. It's a rather lovely old manor house. Large, without being too huge. Masses of character.'

'Is there anything you don't know?' Tara quipped.

'Well, I don't know when or where he was born or who his parents were or what he had for breakfast — but enough of that. That's by the by. Much more importantly, are you allowed to bring a plus one?'

'No. It's purely business.'

'You mean there'll be more like him there?'

'I have no idea, but I assume it's chiefly for employees, so we can exchange ideas and tactics to drum up business. Totally boring, I would imagine.'

Bel eyed her friend, visibly sceptical about that response. 'Yeah, right! With that gorgeous individual to look at? Who're you kidding?'

Tara laughed. Bel was nothing if not outspoken. But that aside, she was also totally lovely to look at. She had no need to envy Tara's figure: tall, five foot eight to Tara's five foot four, and with the sort of willowy figure Tara would die for. Her hair was a glorious auburn, curly but not too curly, and long, cascading down her back to well beneath her shoulders. This, combined with aqua-coloured eyes, a heart-shaped face, and a voluptuous mouth — which owed nothing to any sort of filler — ensured she was never without admirers. It all made Tara feel like a fat midget alongside of her.

They'd known each other since they were five years old. Having begun school on the same day, within hours they'd become firm friends, and had remained that way ever since. So Tara forgave Bel everything. She couldn't imagine life without her. Bel was the one she ran to with her problems, and it was Bel who invariably came up with the right answer.

Bel slanted a glance at her now. 'It sounds as if you haven't taken to him.'

'I didn't.' However, the tinge of pink that she felt creeping up her face had Bel snorting with disbelief.

'Yeah, right,' Bel crowed. 'You fancy

him, don't you?'

Tara belatedly became aware of her co-workers staring their way. 'Sssh,' she hissed. 'And no, I don't. He's a bit too full-on for me. Too sure of himself by half; and as I've already said, totally ruthless to boot. If he's not happy with our performance — or profitability — over the past few months, I don't give one iota for my chances of remaining on as manager.'

'Well then, there's your chance. His drinks party.'

Tara raised a quizzical eyebrow.

'Charm him.'

'I'm not into charming millionaires. It's not my thing.'

'Well, step aside then and leave it to the expert. Take me along with you. He probably won't even notice I wasn't invited — not with all the people likely to be there. I can put your case very subtly.'

'No. And subtle is definitely not your speciality.'

Bel pulled a face. 'Spoilsport.'

Tara was tempted to confide her worries about Ricky to her friend and get her take on things, as she would normally have done. But this time something, a sense of caution perhaps, stopped her. The fewer people who knew he could possibly be a thief, the better; and her friend could be a chatterbox, as Tara had learnt to her cost over the years, with Bel embarrassing her more than once in front of others.

★ ★ ★

Once her friend had gone, Tara settled down to some serious computer work. She was determined that Gray Madison would have the figures he needed before next Wednesday. At the moment, things didn't look too bad. In fact, it looked as if there could be a reasonable profit for last month, and it wasn't looking too grim for March at the present time either. But would that be enough to save her and subsequently the salon? And, more importantly, would it continue over the coming months? Because that was what they needed — a degree of financial stability in order to guarantee a future for them all.

That question hung over her for the rest of the day; that and the other all-important question of where her brother might be. In the end, she was glad to leave work and head for home. She refused to consider whether Ricky would be there or not; she'd abandoned her attempts to contact him for the moment, as it was clearly a complete waste of time. He'd be in touch sooner or later; most likely when he ran out of money. She wasn't going to worry about him any longer. As the police-woman had pointed out, he was a grown man, and well able to take care of himself.

She stopped off at Lizzie's and collected her niece. Daisy, as was her habit, chattered excitedly all the way home, relaying blow by blow all that had happened to her during the day. And even when they walked towards the front door, the flow of words didn't slow.

It wasn't until Tara fitted the key into the lock, and the door opened without her turning it, that the notion that Ricky was possibly back entered her head. But — she swung and looked behind her — his car wasn't there.

'Daisy . . . ' She grabbed the little girl by the shoulder, holding her back as a stab of alarm pierced her. This wasn't Ricky. Someone else had been here. The question was, who? And could whoever it was still be inside?

4

Tara swept a glance around before turning back and briefly examining the door. It had to be someone skilled in picking locks, she reasoned, because the door was completely undamaged. Which suggested a criminal of some sort. One of Ricky's mates? The man who'd phoned her? That seemed the most likely answer. Especially as he'd sounded pretty desperate to get back whatever it was he'd maintained Ricky had taken.

Gingerly, and with a heart that was thudding hard, Tara stepped into the hallway, and immediately saw all the coats that were normally hung in a cupboard lying in a tangled heap on the floor. Slowly, soundlessly, she inched her way around them, still holding on to Daisy, keeping the little girl behind her.

'What's wrong?' Daisy whispered. 'Why are the coats lying on the floor?'

They walked into the kitchen, which was in an even worse state of disorder than the hallway.

'Auntie Tara,' Daisy whimpered, 'what's happened?'

Tara stared around the small room. Cupboards and drawers had been emptied, again all over the floor. The fridge-freezer door was open, as was the oven door. 'Stay here,' she instructed Daisy. She didn't need to say anything more, as the child stood, transfixed, unmoving.

Tara dashed into the sitting room. It was the same there. Shelves swept bare, the ornaments that had been on them lying, a couple broken, on the floor, with cushions from the furniture scattered on the carpet. Armchairs were overturned. The contents from the two cupboards each side of the chimney breast were also scattered over the floor. At first glance, nothing seemed to be missing, yet someone had carried out a thorough search — for whatever it was Ricky had stolen, she guessed.

Daisy came into the room behind her. 'Is this Daddy?' She began to cry. 'Did Daddy do this? Where is he?' She swung and ran from the room, rapidly climbing the stairs, and crying all the way, 'Daddy; Daddy, are you up there?'

Tara leapt after her. The intruder could still be upstairs.

'Daisy — stop. This isn't Daddy's doing.'

She grabbed Daisy's hand and together they went on up. Tara listened all the way but could hear no sound. Whoever this had been had clearly gone. The three rooms, when they got to them, were all in a similar state to downstairs, thoroughly ransacked. Even the bathroom had been searched, with towels and the contents of the two cupboards scattered over the floor. And whoever it had been would have had plenty of time in which to do it. Most of the neighbours would have been out at work. Hardly anyone would have been around to notice someone breaking in. Certainly not the old lady three doors down. She was virtually blind and almost completely disabled.

It could only logically be one person: the man who'd phoned her. He'd been searching for whatever it was that Ricky had taken. Had he found it? She hoped he had, because then he'd surely leave them alone. That still, however, left Ricky missing with no clue as to his present whereabouts.

Daisy slipped her hand from Tara's and ran back into her own bedroom. Tara followed. 'Look, Auntie Tara, look. My dolls, my games — they're all spoilt.' Her voice shook with distress.

'No, sweetie, they're not spoilt, just untidy.' As Daisy had said, everything was strewn around the floor; boxes of games and jigsaws had been opened and their contents scattered haphazardly. Her books and paints lay everywhere. Several dolls had been flung down amongst it all. Even the bed had been stripped, and the mattress, quilt and pillow were on the floor, the same as in the other two rooms. The entire house was a mess.

It would take more than an hour or two to sort out.

But what had the intruder been looking for? Money? Was that what her brother had taken? Or the proceeds of a robbery? Jewellery, antiques? But Tara was sure she would have known if they'd been stashed here somewhere, surely; it was she who tidied and cleaned. She'd have found them. No, it was most likely to be money. Quite a lot in large-denomination notes could be hidden in a fairly small space. But Ricky wouldn't have run off and left any substantial amount behind, so if that was what it was, he must have it with him. Surely, whoever had done this would have known that?

Or had someone else, in turn, stolen it from him and maybe left him injured somewhere? It would explain why he hadn't returned home.

Her mind was spinning almost out of control. The possibilities were endless.

Oh God, Ricky, what have you done? And where the hell are you?

Tara returned to her own room and stood looking around before moving to check whether anything was missing. Her jewellery was all there, not that there was anything of value; not really. Her mother's engagement and wedding rings were still in their boxes, albeit tossed onto the floor amongst everything else.

As she'd already decided, this was no run-of-the-mill burglary. Whoever this was knew exactly what they were looking for. Again, she prayed he'd found it.

She plumped down on the stripped bed and looked around at the mess. Her clothes had been pulled from all the drawers as well as the wardrobe, and then heaped in a pile on the floor along with everything that had been sitting on her dressing table. Her cleansing lotions, her makeup, her perfume, her hairbrush and dryer were all scattered carelessly around. There was no actual damage done to anything, but even so, she didn't know where to start. One thing she did know, however, was that her room and Daisy's would take priority; Ricky's could wait. Maybe he'd return soon, and then he could damned well do his own tidying. Not that she held out much hope of that, even if he did return within the next day or two.

She sighed. She could hear Daisy muttering to herself in the next room as she struggled to restore some sort of order to her belongings. Tara went in to her. Tears were pouring down the little girl's round cheeks, yet she was making no sound. It tore at Tara's heart. If this was down to Ricky, she'd never forgive him; never.

She knelt down and pulled the small weeping girl into her arms. 'Leave it all for now, darling. Let's get some supper. We'll sort this later — together.'

Daisy didn't speak for long moment, her expression much too serious for a five-year-old. Then, 'Are you sure Daddy didn't do this?'

And what else could she say but, 'No, he wouldn't.'

'Then where is he?'

★ ★ ★

After a cursory tidy-up of the kitchen and sitting room, Tara prepared their supper of fish fingers and chips, which they ate in front of the television. Normally she encouraged her niece to sit at the kitchen table and eat, but this evening, given the circumstances, she forgot the rules. Anything to distract Daisy from what was happening.

Eventually, of course, they had to set to and tidy up, at least basically. Tara remade their beds, and together they restored all of Daisy's toys and games to their rightful places. However, the jigsaws were a different matter. All the pieces had been jumbled together; they'd have to leave those for another day. Tara did fleetingly think that whatever had been stolen couldn't be very large if it could be fitted into games and jigsaw boxes. Which she supposed could indicate jewellery. You would be able to fit quite a large amount of valuable rings and necklaces

70

into those. But would Ricky have done such a thing — and to his daughter? Especially when there was always the risk that Daisy would open a box and discover the items. Surely the intruder would have realised that?

By the time they'd done what they could, Daisy was pale-faced with exhaustion.

'Come on,' Tara tenderly said, 'let's get you to bed. You've got school tomorrow.'

Daisy, for once, didn't argue. Once she was tucked in, she pleaded, 'Can I have a story — ple-ease?'

'Just one, then.'

But she didn't even manage to stay awake for that. Tara tenderly kissed her velvety cheek before going to her own room to tidy. The rest of the house would have to wait until the following day. She, too, was exhausted. She'd get up early and do what she had to then. More than anything, she desperately wanted things to return to normal, and forget this had ever happened.

But that wasn't to be.

Against all the odds, she managed to get Daisy to school on time and then continued on to the salon, where completely unexpectedly, she was confronted with the same scene of chaos she'd faced at home the evening before.

The contents of the many cupboards and drawers had been turned out onto the floor. Chairs were tipped over, the reception desk ransacked, the couches in the two treatment rooms stripped and moved. Even the small restroom-cum-office and toilet had been searched. Yet once again, nothing seemed to have been stolen.

It had to be the same person responsible. But what on earth had Ricky taken? And why would the intruder have thought it might be at his sister's salon? It had to be money or jewellery, things that could be fairly easily concealed. There was no other explanation. But again, whatever it was, it could have been discovered by one of the staff.

All Tara knew was, things were

starting to feel scary; really scary. Ricky must have talked about her to whoever this was. Which led her to ask herself what this person would do next. Confront her? Threaten her if she didn't tell him what she knew? The trouble was, she knew nothing.

The doorbell tinged, and she glanced around to see Annie standing there staring around in horror.

'What the hell's happened here? Did a bomb explode?'

'No. Just a break-in.'

'Just a — ? Oh my God. What's missing?'

'Nothing, as far as I can see.'

'Nothing?' Annie shook her head, visibly confused.

'It's probably kids, bored and looking for entertainment.'

'Going a bit far, isn't it? And how did they get in? There's no visible damage to the door or window.' She'd bent over and was closely examining the lock on the door.

'The lock's been picked,' Tara told her.

'And how would mere kids know how to do that? Normally they'd just smash a window.' Annie was starting to look puzzled; suspicious, even.

Tara shrugged, her mind moving into overdrive. Annie was pretty sharp and wouldn't be easily fooled. She'd know there was more to this than mere kids' mischief. 'They can find out how to do anything on YouTube. How to make firebombs, anything. I'm pretty sure picking a lock would be covered.'

She gnawed at her bottom lip. She'd been meaning to get the lock changed to a mortise lock for a while. Sadly, she hadn't got round to it. She'd have to now. Here and at the house. The trouble was, neither had seemed particularly urgent. Mallow End had always been a relatively crime-free town.

Annie had removed her keen-eyed gaze from Tara and was looking around at the mess. 'Well, we'd better clear up, and pretty darned quickly. The first appointment is in . . . ' She checked her wristwatch. ' . . . half an hour.'

The door opened again, this time to admit the other members of staff. Their reactions were identical to Annie's.

'Bloomin' 'eck. What's happened here, then?'

With all of them working swiftly and efficiently, the salon was soon restored to order, just in time. The first client appeared as they were putting away the last few items.

Despite Annie's desire to call the police, Tara prevaricated. 'No point. They won't be interested. Nothing's been taken, and there's no real damage.'

Apart from a low murmuring of, 'Well, I think we should,' she accepted Tara's thumbs-down and instead got down to work.

★   ★   ★

The following few days passed busily and quickly, bolstering Tara's hopes that she would have some good profit figures to show Gray Madison.

The only ripple to disturb her optimistic outlook was Ricky's failure to reappear; and despite her resolve to not worry any more about him, she couldn't shake off her fear that some sort of harm might have come to him. Or, failing that, he might simply have got himself involved with a gang of criminals. Because of that possibility, she couldn't bring herself to report him still missing to the police. An official investigation might uncover the fact that he'd been involved in some sort of theft, and what then? He could very well find himself behind bars.

But then, on the following Monday evening, she was getting ready to go to bed when she happened to glance out of the bedroom window while she was drawing the curtains and noticed a car parked on the opposite side of the road, strategically outside of the beam of any streetlight. She could just about make out that someone was sitting inside, in the driver's seat. The headlights weren't on and the engine wasn't running. It was obviously parked.

Tara frowned. The driver must be waiting for someone. But at ten thirty at night, in a residential area? She couldn't help wondering how long the vehicle had been there. Had it been there before, on another night, and she hadn't noticed it? A prickling of apprehension made itself felt. Could this, too, be connected to Ricky's disappearance — eight days ago now? If it wasn't, it was a pretty huge coincidence.

She drew back so that she was partially concealed by the curtain, but the driver obviously spotted her because he — she could see, even in the darkness, that it was a man — leant forward and stared directly up at her.

She darted backwards — he was watching her! Watching the house. Well, that seemed to answer her question. He was waiting for Ricky to return.

Her breathing quickened. Her throat dried.

No, surely it must be coincidence. Because if he was waiting for Ricky, what would happen when — if — he returned?

She recalled the threat he'd made on the phone. 'I'll take something of Ricky's.' Did he mean her? Was that why he was outside of the house? No, she was being stupid now. 'Oh, Ricky,' she groaned. 'What the hell have you done?'

Eventually she forced herself to look back through the window, and to her relief, she saw that the car had gone. It must have been coincidence. Nothing to do with Ricky or her. But still, there'd been that look — straight up at her.

She climbed into bed, only to lie awake, events endlessly — crazily — spiralling in her head. Dawn was lightening the sky before she fell asleep.

★ ★ ★

By the time Wednesday evening arrived, and there'd been no further sighting of the mystery car, Tara's fears began to ease. However, they pretty damn quickly resurrected themselves as she began to get ready for Gray Madison's party. Why oh why had she agreed to go? It was the very last thing she needed right now. She had more than enough on her plate as it was.

She sighed heavily. It was too late to cancel, so she had no option. She had to go. After all, her job could be at stake.

Lizzie had agreed to babysit and would be here in half an hour, so she needed to get a move on. Frowning, she regarded the heap of discarded garments on her bed. There was nothing suitable for what she suspected would be quite a stylish party. She really needed to buy herself a few new things, but between work and looking after Daisy, she didn't have much free time.

Oh, to hell with it. He'd have to take her as she came. She swiftly sorted through the pile once more and pulled out a black skirt and a pale blue silky blouse, neither of which she'd worn for some time. She held them up and scanned them. They'd do. She was just an employee after all, not a guest as such. In fact, the occasion could be regarded as a works party, she supposed. With that, she immediately felt better.

She slipped her arms into the blouse sleeves and fastened the buttons at the front. A fleeting glance into the mirror, however, showed her a blouse that was gaping badly, pulled tight as it was over her full breasts. Trying to ignore that fact — she could always wear a scarf over it — she pulled on a pair of black opaque tights and then the skirt. But — oh no, that was too tight as well. The fastener would barely close, and it was too short to boot. She stared down over herself and then back into the mirror. The skirt finished a good five or six inches above her knees. Had it always been that short? She didn't think so. She'd put on weight, she must have. She'd swear neither garment had been this snug the last time she'd worn them.

She looked awful. Thoroughly exasperated by now, she tore the clothes off. Now what?

The only possibility was a sapphire-blue lace shift dress. It wasn't as snug a fit as the skirt and blouse, but it did sport a low neckline and a fairly high hemline. However, it was an improvement on the first outfit. Mind you, anything would be an improvement on that. She considered her reflection, her head to one side. Might it be a bit dressy for what she'd already decided would be a works 'do'?

She sighed. Beggars couldn't be choosers. It would have to do, but she resolved to make time for a spot of shopping within the next couple of weeks to purchase some new garments. She then exchanged the black tights for some navy-blue hold-up stockings, and made an attempt to conceal the inches of cleavage on display with a chunky three-strand necklace. The only problem was that the large round beads were extraordinarily heavy, and after an hour or so, she usually felt weighed down and suffering from backache into the bargain.

She quickly brushed her hair. It could have done with a shampoo to give it some body, but she simply didn't have the time. She was in the process of shrugging on a jacket when her doorbell chimed. Lizzie.

She ran down the stairs and opened the door. Daisy was still up and watching television in the sitting room. Upon hearing the bell, she ran into the hallway and flung herself at Lizzie.

Lizzie stared at Tara and said, 'You look nice. Where did you say you were going?'

'My new boss's drinks party. Gray Madison. It's at his house in Abbotsleigh.' She pulled a wry face at her friend. 'Do I look okay? I wasn't sure what —'

'Do you look okay?' Lizzie echoed. 'You look flippin' gorgeous. He'll give you an immediate pay rise, I shouldn't wonder.'

'I wish. I've put weight on,' Tara

groaned. 'Everything's too tight.'

'Well, if you have, it's gone on in all the right places, believe me.'

★   ★   ★

Tara's unease intensified the nearer she got to Abbotsleigh and Osborne House. What sort of people would be there? Mere employees like her, or managers and directors? Thinking about it, a drinks party suggested something rather grand with canapés and the like. She nibbled at her bottom lip, fervently wishing she hadn't agreed to come. This sentiment was instantly reinforced when she saw the grandeur of the wrought-iron gates that confronted her at the entrance to the house; they towered above her car and must be ten feet high, at least. Then, as if that wasn't enough, she spotted the house itself, and she was tempted to turn around right there and then and go home again.

The house was even grander than the

gates had seemed to suggest. It was two storeys high and constructed in honey-coloured brickwork with a slate roof and a regiment of tall, ornate chimney pots. The sheer number of stone mullioned windows — she counted thirty in all across the front — hinted at a great many rooms, both upstairs and on the ground floor. The solid oak front door was positioned at the top of a short flight of steps and was flanked by impressive stone columns. It had the look of a large period rectory, the sort of house a family from a Jane Austin novel would have inhabited. The Bennets, maybe.

She stared up at it as she climbed from the car. It was all massively attractive, and the sort of house that only someone extremely wealthy would own. There was some sort of climbing plant scrambling up the brickwork. Lights were blazing from several windows, and arc lights illuminated the entire frontage, as well as several expensive-looking cars, along with half a dozen similar to her own — small and cheap — which did provide a modicum of reassurance. She wouldn't be alone with the rich and prosperous, then.

Knowing she couldn't go for the overwhelmingly tempting option of simply turning round and going home, not if she wanted to keep her job, Tara straightened her shoulders and climbed the stone steps. She had raised one hand to press the bell when the door unexpectedly opened, and there stood Gray Madison himself.

Tara was startled. She'd expected some sort staff member; a housekeeper, maybe. She didn't think even Gray Madison would employ a butler.

He smiled down at her, his amber gaze raking her from the top of her head right down to her feet, it seemed. 'Ah, Ms Wyndham,' he finally said. 'So glad you could come.'

'Well,' Tara murmured, 'I said I would.'

'Quite. Well, come in and let me take your jacket.'

She stepped into what looked like a marble-floored hallway that was spacious enough to contain practically the entire ground floor of her own house and handed her jacket to him. Again, she was acutely aware of his glance skimming over her, as well as the glint of — what? Could it be admiration? A sensation of warmth spread through her — until she noticed his casual mode of dress, that was. An open neck, tan shirt and cream chino trousers. She swallowed. She was over-dressed, just as she'd feared. Well, it was too late to do anything about it now.

Holding her breath, she followed him into a large and very luxuriously furnished sitting room, fully expecting to see everyone else dressed equally as casually.

5

A fleeting glance around the room, however, showed a more or less equal split between smart casual and dressy. Tara allowed herself a small breath of relief.

Gray slanted a glance at her. Had he heard? If he had, he gave no indication of it. 'Let me introduce you,' was all he said.

Tara estimated there were a couple of dozen people in the room, each one holding a flute of champagne. A woman appeared at her side; she was dressed formally in a black skirt and white blouse, and was holding a tray full of glasses. Another followed dressed in exactly the same uniform, this one bearing a large platter of exotic-looking canapés. Tara hid a smile. Thank goodness her own black skirt and pale blue blouse hadn't fitted her. If they had, she'd have very likely been mistaken for one of the waitresses. And that would have been truly humiliating.

She helped herself to one of the flutes, but refused a canapé. It was a drink she needed, and quickly. A swig of alcohol hopefully would calm her twitching nerves. Not that she intended drinking more than a glassful of anything. She had to drive home, after all.

'Tara,' Gray said, touching her arm, 'this is Jennifer.'

Tara swung to meet the cool gaze of an attractive woman. No lack of confidence there. Maybe she wasn't an employee, but a friend; girlfriend, even?

But no. Gray went on, 'She's in charge of the Worcester salon. Jennifer, Tara is at Mallow End.'

'Oh yes, I know it. Mine's considerably larger, of course. We have a hairdressing service as well, so a bit more of a challenge. How are you finding business?'

Despite the question, Jennifer didn't

sound all that interested. In fact, she made no attempt to hide her lack of curiosity — other than for a scornful glance at Tara's generous display of cleavage. Just as she made no attempt to hide her certainty of her own superiority.

'Good; yes, good.' Even to Tara's own ears, her words didn't sound convincing. Jennifer clearly detected the same thing, because she made no attempt to hide her scepticism. She arched a pair of immaculately shaped eyebrows, obviously having made full use of her own salon's services.

'You do surprise me,' she went on in the same superior fashion. 'Mallow End's rather nondescript, not to say small, isn't it? I mean, do the inhabitants even know what aromatherapy is?' And she slanted a disdainful smile Gray's way — as if to say, 'Why are you wasting your time on her?'

In light of this, and determined to put both her and Gray right, Tara went on, 'Oh, goodness me — yes. We might be small, but . . . '

But Jennifer had already turned her head away to murmur something into Gray's ear; something disparaging about her, no doubt. To Gray's credit, however, he didn't respond.

Tara, thoroughly incensed by this behaviour, tightened her lips. The other woman couldn't have made her contempt more obvious. She took another much-needed swig of her champagne.

When Gray still didn't respond to her, Jennifer, looking more than a little miffed, drifted away. He then turned to Tara and said, 'Come and meet Maddie. Her salon's the same size approximately as yours.' Although he didn't say so, she sensed his disapproval of the way Jennifer had spoken to her, and surprisingly, that went some way towards reassuring Tara about the future of her salon.

It took a few more minutes to meet the rest of the guests. They weren't all in the beauty business. There were several from the other concerns that Gray was involved in. Tara wasn't sure what they were, but she was sure she'd pretty soon find out.

One man, Mark Bellamy — he managed a DIY store on the fringe of Birmingham, Homes and Gardens, one of another nationwide chain that Gray Madison presumably owned, otherwise why would he be here this evening? — showed a bit too much interest in Tara; in particular, her cleavage. His gaze repeatedly drifted to it. However, unlike Jennifer's, his expression was one of unabashed admiration. Clearly, her chunky beads were providing no protection at all. But what made the whole thing even worse was that Gray noticed too. His eyes and jaw hardened; so much so that Mark eventually noticed, and a dull flush reddened his face.

'Right.' Gray abruptly took hold of her elbow and steered her away. 'Just one left. My business partner, Cameron McKenzie.'

Cameron, she guessed, was about the same age as Gray, mid-thirties? He wasn't as good-looking as Gray, but he exuded a charm and warmth that were exceedingly attractive. He gave Tara a lazy smile as he held out a well-groomed hand.

'Good to meet you, Tara. Gray's spoken about you.'

Had he? Tara dared a glance at Gray, and saw that once again his expression had hardened as he regarded the other man. Why would Gray have spoken about her — unless it was to name her salon as one of the ones they planned to close? Her heart lurched with dismay.

'I talk about all my businesses — and employees,' he pointedly elaborated, swivelling his head to regard Cameron from eyes that now glinted with minute gold specks. Tara wondered if that signified anger, or something else entirely.

Cameron appeared totally unfazed, however, drawling, 'So you do, old man. He's very much a hands-on boss, so be warned, Tara.' And he strolled away, glass in hand, chuckling to himself.

Tara eyed Gray nervously in the wake of this. Was that exasperation that quirked his lips, or amusement? The latter, most likely. And what the hell did Cameron mean by 'very much a hands-on boss, so be warned'? Hands on what, exactly? She felt her face warming.

'Ignore Cameron. He was making mischief, something he frequently does, primarily to wind me up,' Gray said in an undertone. 'I'll leave you to circulate and make the acquaintance of some of the other guests in more depth. You should talk some more to Maddie; you'll have lots in common.' And he too moved away.

She watched him go, gnawing at her bottom lip, and asking herself whether she'd annoyed him in some way; but she couldn't think how. She'd barely opened her mouth since she'd first walked in. Yet Gray seemed extremely keen to leave her. She stood now, sipping at her champagne and looking around the room, trying not to resemble that most embarrassing of things — the wallflower that no one wanted to talk to.

The room was really very stylish and beautiful, with its discreet lighting and duck-egg blue, apricot and ivory walls; its cream deep-cushioned furniture; its blue carpet, a shade deeper than the walls. There were several pieces of antique furniture, tables and cabinets, and the walls were hung with what looked like extremely expensive art, each piece again subtly illuminated.

'You look lonely. Mind if I join you?'

It was Mark. 'No, not at all,' she gushed — only to go on and say, 'I'm feeling a bit like the duckling that everyone ignored. The ugly one.' Oh no, why had she said that? He'd now think she was angling for a compliment. She needed to slow down her consumption of the champagne. She'd had her glass topped up once already.

And, true to expected form, Mark didn't disappoint. 'I can assure you that no one would consider you ugly. You're lovely, but I'm sure you've been told that many times.' His smouldering gaze skimmed over her, all of her, once again lingering on her exposed cleavage.

'I haven't, actually.'

'I'm sure you're being too modest.'

'No, I'm not, believe me. I don't often get the opportunity to go out and meet people, so . . . ' She stopped talking, unable to believe the words that were pouring from her mouth. She clamped it tightly shut, at the same time glaring at the by-now almost empty glass in her hand. Had she really drunk all of that? Even as she had the thought, a waitress topped her up yet again. Heavens above, at this rate she was going to be well and truly drunk by the time she left.

Mark rolled his eyes at her. 'Now you're sounding like Cinderella. Don't tell me you have a wicked stepmother at home.'

'No, just a small niece who takes up the better part of my time.'

'A niece? But surely her mother — ?' He looked puzzled.

'Well, that's the problem. Her mother

doesn't figure in her life.'

'A father, then?' He was studying her intently now.

'The same. He's not around much either — actually, not at all at the moment.'

'So where is he? Where are they both, come to that?'

She shrugged, unconsciously exposing even more inches of creamy flesh. His gaze again flew to the unintended display, and she distinctly heard his soft intake of breath. Her face warmed, especially when she saw that she was also being closely observed by Gray Madison, who was standing, glass in hand, watching her every move from beneath heavily lidded eyes. Instinctively she half turned to face Mark fully once more, and away from Gray. He was still talking; she simply hadn't been listening. Without thinking, she took another hefty mouthful of the champagne from the glass that had been miraculously refilled.

'Sorry — what?'

'I asked, where's her father? Would that be your brother?'

'Yes. He has this unfortunate habit of disappearing every now and again.'

She tried to make light of this, but Mark's expression clearly showed his disapproval. 'Leaving you holding the baby — literally?'

'Quite.'

'So how old is this baby?'

'Five — going on eighteen.'

'And who's with her tonight?'

'A babysitter.'

His expression of disapproval evaporated. 'So would this babysitter oblige again? So that I could take you out?'

'Everything okay here?'

Tara swivelled, somewhat unsteadily she was dismayed to note, to discover Gray standing just behind them. Neither she nor Mark had noticed his approach. How long had he been standing there? Could he be hoping to overhear some sort of indiscretion?

'Fine, boss.' Mark laughed. 'Going rather well, actually.' He winked at Tara.

She saw Gray stiffen right before he said, 'There's someone over there keen to talk to you, Mark.' He indicated a man standing in the far corner of the room.

'Oh God, it's Ray Compton,' he muttered. He glanced sideways at Tara. 'Sorry. It's a supplier, one of our biggest. I didn't realise he'd be here. I thought it was just employees.' He turned back to Tara. 'Look, give me your number and I'll ring you.'

'That won't be necessary,' Gray unceremoniously cut in. 'I've got Tara's number. I'll let you have it.'

Tara stared at him. 'You've got my number?'

'Yes, of course. The salon number.'

'Oh, yes, of course.' Now she sounded — and felt — stupid; naive, even. Of course he'd have the salon number. What had she thought, that he'd have her private number? Why would he?

'It was her private number I was after, actually,' Mark persisted.

'Another time, Mark,' Gray said. 'I

wish to discuss something with Tara now.'

'Right. Well, here's my card.' Mark thrust it at her. 'Ring me and we'll fix something up.'

Tara took it and glanced at it. It had his private numbers as well as his business number. 'O-kay.'

The second Mark had left them, Gray said, 'It might be wise to steer clear of him — Mark.'

'Why's that, then?' She widened her eyes at him.

He took a deep breath, a not altogether steady breath — she wondered if he'd also had a little too much champagne — and said, 'He's a bit of a womaniser.'

'Really?' She was about to add, 'I've heard the same thing about you,' before deciding that might not be altogether wise. He was her employer, after all. So instead, she asked, 'What do you want to discuss?'

'I was wondering whether you've brought the salon's figures up to date yet?'

'Yes. I emailed them to the Birmingham office, as I usually do.'

'Oh, right — good. I'll have a look at them.'

Which begged the question — why had he pushed her for them if he couldn't be bothered to look at them?

Her expression must have revealed her thoughts, because he went on, 'I haven't been into the office this week.'

Which was a strange thing to say. He could access them, surely, from his home computer?

'I've been rather busy — out of the country for several days. So have they improved?'

'Improving, certainly. As I mentioned during your visit, we've had a lot of walk-in clients.'

'Hmm, but that's not really reliable, is it? They could disappear overnight. It's a regular clientele you want, booking appointments on a weekly, or at the very least, a monthly basis.'

'We've got those too. Not so many on a weekly basis, but the monthlies are pretty steady.'

'Okay. Well, maybe . . . ' He went on

to discuss some sort of local promotional campaign.

In return, Tara told him about her mail shots. 'I'm planning on doing that on a regular basis.'

'Good; I like a display of initiative, but it needs to be a bigger effort, covering a wider radius. Now, how about some food? There's a buffet laid out in the dining room.'

'Good idea.' She regarded her champagne glass — empty again — with dismay. Where had that disappeared to? She hadn't been conscious of drinking it, but clearly she had. Which was why the swimming of her head was telling her to eat something — and quickly.

'Come along, then. I'll show you.'

It was as they were crossing the hallway that Jennifer accosted them. 'Gray, do you have a moment?'

She pouted her full and visibly botoxed lips, forcing Tara to hide a smile. The other woman obviously thought the gesture sexy, when in reality all if did was make her look like a trout. Oh dear, Tara mused, that was a little cruel of her.

'There's something I need to ask you,' Jennifer went on, turning her back on Tara.

'Will you excuse me, Tara?' Gray said, his expression one of mute apology. 'The dining room's through there.' He indicated an open door across the hall.

Tara simply nodded. Honestly, what was Jennifer's problem? If she thought that Tara had any sort of romantic interest in Gray, she couldn't be more mistaken. She'd as soon get involved with a man-eating tiger.

She was loading a plate full of irresistible goodies when she became aware of Mark once more at her side.

'Now, where were we?' The words were a low, throaty murmur.

'I don't remember,' Tara bluntly told him. She didn't wish to encourage him. Although moderately handsome, he really wasn't her type. Of medium height, not actually overweight, but could certainly benefit from losing a couple of pounds, and with a slightly florid face, she felt no real attraction to him.

'You were about to give me your phone number.'

'Was I?' She hadn't been, but not wishing to be rude and refuse, she obliged.

He pulled out a mobile phone and entered the number she gave him. 'Great. I'll ring you.'

Hoping to discourage him, she said, 'Well, as I told you, it's a bit difficult to get out in the evenings.'

Her words had no effect upon him at all. 'Oh, I'm sure that between us, we'll be able to sort something out. Now, tell me all about yourself.' He gave her an irritatingly smug smile.

By the time ten o'clock came round, Tara decided she'd had way too much to drink to risk driving home, due — she attempted to excuse her own part in things — to the sheer boredom of having to listen to one anecdote after another of Mark's supposedly comical experiences over the years. Deep down, though, she knew it wasn't entirely his fault. She'd heedlessly used the consumption of too much alcohol to allay her unease at being here, in the house of the man who held her fate firmly in his hands.

Finally she'd succeeded in escaping Mark, but only by locking herself into the loo and staying there. She'd had to come out in the end, of course, when someone had repeatedly knocked on the door, calling, 'Are you okay in there?'

'S-sorry,' she'd muttered as she exited. 'Upset tummy.'

Nonetheless, her tactic had worked. Mark was now boring some other poor woman to tears, if the expression on her face was any guide. Tara glanced around the room, wondering if she could make a quick and discreet getaway. She could call a taxi once she was outside, and no one would realise how intoxicated she was. That intention was foiled, however, when she noticed that Gray had spotted her standing alone in the corner of the room. She noticed he was with Jennifer again. Like Mark with regards to herself, Jennifer was seemingly determined to capture and hold Gray's attention.

But, also like Mark, her flirtatious behaviour wasn't getting her anywhere. Tara watched as Gray bent his head towards her and said something. She saw Jennifer turn her head and look across the room at her, the expression in her eyes one of undiluted loathing. And then Gray was striding across the room, his intention clearly to speak to Tara.

Well, here was her chance. She'd ask him to call a taxi for her. He'd be bound to know a local firm.

'Tara? Are you all right?'

'I'm fine. Um, I have to go.'

'Do you? Why? It's early yet.' He didn't sound pleased.

'I have to get back for the babysitter.'

Both eyebrows lifted at this nugget of information. 'Babysitter? You have a child?'

'Oh, no. She's my niece. My brother's daughter, Daisy.'

'I see. He's not at home, then, to look after her?'

'Uh, no.' She shrugged, not offering any sort of explanation. Her private life wasn't any of his business, anyway.

But whether it was or not, his glance sharpened with what looked dangerously like displeasure. 'I was hoping to have the chance of another word.'

'S-sorry. Maybe you could call me at the salon — ? Um — I-I wonder, could you call me a taxi?' She gave a rueful smile. 'I've had a little too much wine to drive.' Huh! A little too much? She'd had about a bucketful too much. She just hoped she didn't appear too intoxicated to the man who was, after all, her boss.

'I could take you home.' The look of displeasure — if that was what it had indeed been — vanished, to be replaced by a disquieting gleam within the amber eyes. For a second, he looked — well, predatory. Maybe he wasn't that far removed from the man-eating tiger she'd mentally compared him to earlier, after all. To her dismay then, a tremor of what could only be described as excitement rippled through her.

'Oh, I wouldn't want to put you to any trouble, and you still have guests.' She indicated the people still standing around the room. From the looks of it, she'd be the first to go.

'Yes, so I do,' he ruefully agreed. 'I'll ring the firm I use when I need to. Their drivers are a hundred percent reliable.'

He tapped in a number on his phone and ordered a car for her. 'I'll get yours returned in the morning if you leave me the key and your address and phone numbers, landline and mobile.'

'Oh, but — really, there's no need.'

'How will you get to work in the morning?'

He was right to ask the question, of course. The salon was a good mile from the house. She could walk, she supposed. But she could already hear

Daisy's protests about that. The school was almost that far away. She handed him her car key and told him her address and phone numbers. He keyed it all into his phone.

By the time this was done, the doorbell was ringing.

'Goodness, that was quick,' she said.

'Yes,' Gray smiled down at her. 'I keep someone on standby when I'm entertaining. Now, your jacket.'

Tara couldn't hide her astonishment. Keep someone on standby? Although why she should be astonished, she didn't know. It was just the sort of thing a man of Gray's standing and wealth would do. Really, these people lived in another world entirely to hers. Another universe, more like. Yet for all that, Gray was obviously a man of many aspects; on the one hand keeping a car on standby for his guests, on the other fetching a jacket for one of those same guests.

He helped her on with it, and then murmured, 'I'll see you out.'

'Oh, no — please, there's no need. I'm sure I can find my way.' However, even as she said it and began to walk away, she stumbled and would almost certainly have fallen if Gray hadn't reached out to catch her and then steady her. 'S-sorry.' As his arm encircled her waist, she felt a blush staining her cheek. Whatever must he be thinking of her? That he was employing a lush to manage one of his salons, probably. Well, there went her job. She'd probably get a letter of some description within the next few days terminating her employment, citing unacceptable behaviour.

'No worries.' He steered her into the hallway and across to the front door. He opened it and then assisted her down the steps. At the bottom, he looked at her, a frown on his brow and asked, 'Will you be all right?'

'Oh, goodness me, yes. You've been very kind, and-and th-thank you for a splendid party.'

She could see he was desperately

trying to conceal a grin. She felt her face warming for a second time. Oh God, she was making things worse and worse. He was laughing at her. Why couldn't she learn to keep her mouth shut at times like these? She tugged her arm from his grasp and started towards the taxi. Yet again, she stumbled. And yet again, he was forced to make a grab for her.

'S-sorry.' That was all she seemed able to say. So not only would he be thinking she was a lush, he'd now have her down as stupid into the bargain. Could things get any worse? At this point, she was visualising her job physically disappearing down a drain.

'That's okay. I'm glad I was here.'

She looked up at him. There was a distinct gleam once again to his eye. Oh yes, he was definitely laughing at her. And when all was said and done, who could blame him? She'd undoubtedly made a complete prat of herself. He'd have her down as a naive, unworldly woman who couldn't take more than a drink or two and then found it well nigh impossible to make it out of the house without his assistance. Why on earth would he continue to employ her and as a manager, to boot? She'd sealed her own fate.

In a desperate but most likely futile attempt to redeem herself and hopefully hang on to her job, she chose her words carefully, and somehow managed to enunciate them without slurring or stammering. 'Well — again, thank you for a very enjoyable evening.'

'I'm glad you had a good time. I'll be in touch.'

She stared at him now. 'W-will you?' *What for?* she almost asked. *To sack me?*

'Oh yes,' he softly said. 'I most certainly will.'

Her heart somersaulted in her breast. 'H-have I done something wrong?'

Again, she had to watch as he struggled not to grin. He was enjoying watching her squirm, the beast.

'No. The exact opposite, as a matter of fact.'

'Oh?'

But vexingly, he said nothing more. Instead, he steered her to the waiting taxi and helped her inside. He then gave the driver her address and handed him something. He watched as the vehicle moved away and exited the gateway into the lane.

★ ★ ★

'We've arrived, love.'

Tara opened her eyes to stare in utter bemusement at the taxi driver. Oh good Lord, could she make matters any worse than they already were? She must have dozed off, despite the fact that the entire journey wouldn't have taken more than a few minutes. Would he tell Gray? Probably, and they'd most likely have a good laugh about it. The perfect end to a not very enjoyable evening, she grimly decided. She gathered her handbag and opened the rear door.

'I should get out this side if I were you.' It was the driver; he'd got out and opened the door on the opposite side to where she'd sat. The pavement side. 'Safer.'

She scrambled across the seat, gratefully accepting the hand he offered. Once she was upright, she opened her handbag, intending to pay him.

'It's okay. 'S already paid for.'

Gray must have paid him. 'Well, thank you.'

''S all right.' He grinned at her. 'Now, do you want a hand in?'

'Oh no, I'll be fine, really.'

'Sure?' He couldn't seem to stop grinning.

'I'm very sure.'

She swung and walked across the pavement towards her own driveway, hell-bent on not stumbling, and thus needing yet another man's assistance. Which meant she didn't notice the black car that had been parked a few yards along the road pulling away once the driver had seen her exit the taxi cab.

6

Lizzie grinned as Tara walked, some-what unsteadily, into the sitting room. 'Bit the worse for wear, are we? Oh no, you didn't drive, did you?' The broad grin vanished and concern took its place.

'Of course not. I took a taxi.'

'That's a relief. B-but where's your car?'

'At Osborne House. Gray's going to get it back to me first thing in the morning.'

'Hmmm. Gray, is it? Interesting.' Mirth once again danced in Lizzie's eyes.

'Well, it is his name.'

'Yes, but I hadn't realised you were on first-name terms already.'

To which Tara had no response. Mainly because her head was beginning to ache, and she was finding it virtually impossible to put her thoughts into any sort of order. Which left her with just one question. 'Has Daisy been okay?'

To her relief, this successfully diverted Lizzie from the topic of the current state of Tara and Gray's relationship. 'She did have a nightmare. She woke up crying and calling for Ricky.'

'Oh God.'

'She told me he's left home and been gone for a while.'

'Ten days. I haven't been able to reach him. He's not picking up his calls.'

Lizzie eyed her. 'Have you reported him as missing to the police?'

'I did phone them, but as it had only been a couple of days at the time, they weren't interested.' She evaded Lizzie's gaze as she said it. How could she tell her — tell anyone, come to that — that she believed Ricky had stolen something from the man who'd phoned her? Which could be the reason he hadn't returned home and wasn't answering his phone. And that was aside from the worry that the police might start investigating him for real and arrest him for theft if she shared her concerns with them.

'Well, ring them again. They've got to take you seriously now, surely?'

'I'd rather not.' She flopped down onto the settee. 'It's not the first time he's stayed away a few days.' Which was partly true. He had stayed away, but never for this long.

'Well, if you're really worried . . . '

'I am, but — '

'But what?'

'I'd prefer not to get the police involved — not yet. I doubt they'll be any more interested than they were in the first place. He's a grown man, not a child. He's entitled to go where he wants when he wants. Anyway, there could be some perfectly reasonable explanation.' She didn't know who she was trying to convince, herself or Lizzie. 'Knowing Ricky, he'll just waltz in, asking what all the panic's about.' She shrugged.

Lizzie got to her feet. 'Well, it's your

decision. I'll get off. I wasn't expecting you this early. Oh, by the way, a car's been parked on the other side of the road for quite a while. A black car, it looked like, although in the dark . . . ' She shrugged. 'It couldn't be Ricky, could it? There was a man sitting in the driver's seat, but I couldn't see clearly enough to identify him. But he'd have come into the house, wouldn't he?'

'Yes, of course he would.' Tara's pulse raced. 'It's not there now; I'd have noticed.' But would she? She went to the window and looked out. No car. But — hang on. She dimly recalled a vehicle moving away from the kerb as she'd climbed out of the taxi. But it was only a vague impression; a movement glimpsed from the corner of her eye. She couldn't actually picture it. Could it have been the same car that she'd spotted a few evenings ago? That had been black, too. If it was, then it could indicate that someone was watching the house; and if that suspicion was correct, it could only mean that Ricky had got himself involved in something serious; serious enough for him to disappear off the radar.

'I just thought I'd mention it, mainly because it seemed strange for someone to sit in a parked car for that long. He must have been there for an hour or an hour and a half. I debated calling the police, but then thought I might be wasting their time, so I left it.'

'Thanks, Lizzie, but I'm sure it's nothing to do with Ricky.'

'Right. Well, just so you know. I'm off, then. I'll see you tomorrow afternoon when you call in for Daisy.'

★ ★ ★

Tara barely slept that night, partly because every time she closed her eyes, the room spun around her. The result was that come morning, her head was thumping fit to burst and her eyes were sore and gritty. That was what came of drinking more than she was accustomed to. She knew what it did to her.

Why had she been so stupid? All she could do was put the entire debacle down to her worry over Ricky. That and the knowledge that her job could be under serious threat. Which belatedly seemed two perfectly good excuses for indulging herself.

A cup of coffee was essential before she was forced to cope with Daisy's spirited chatter. She'd swear the child barely drew breath between words.

'Daisy,' she eventually called up the stairs, 'time to get up and get ready for school.'

'I'm not feeling very well,' Daisy called back. 'I don't want to go.'

'Sweetheart, you have to. I need to go to work.'

She climbed the stairs and went into her niece's room. 'You look fine. What's wrong?'

'It's my tummy. It's sore.'

Tara crossed the room to the bed and laid a hand on the little girl's forehead. It was cool, no sign of a higher than normal temperature. Her eyes were their customary bright blue, and her complexion was the usual colour, peaches and cream.

'Well, everything looks fine, so come on; chop, chop.'

'Don't want to.' Daisy burrowed beneath her quilt, yanking it up and over her head.

'Daisy, please. I have to go to the salon. You're perfectly well, so come on.' Tara eyed her then. 'What lessons do you have today?'

'Spelling test,' she muttered.

Ah. That explained it. Daisy hated the weekly spelling test. 'Well, how else will you learn to spell? You don't want to be someone who can't, do you? What will people think if you can't write properly?'

'Don't care what they think,' she grumbled.

Eventually, Tara persuaded her out of bed and down the stairs — just as she heard the sound of a car engine outside. She went to the kitchen window and saw her car pulling up. Well, two cars actually. A man climbed from hers and walked to the front door. She hurried to open it.

'Ms Wyndham?'

'That's me.'

'Your key.' He held it out to her.

'Thank you so much.' She felt her face flame as she wondered if he knew the real reason for his errand this morning.

'No trouble. Mr Madison would have come himself, but he had an early breakfast meeting.'

Tara drew a breath of relief. She'd have been tempted to run and hide if it had been Gray standing on her doorstep. Lord knew what he must have thought the evening before, when she said she needed a taxi. That she was a drunk, probably, as she dimly recalled thinking at the time. She wondered, also not for the first time, whether her reckless behaviour would jeopardise her job.

The man smiled at her; there was no hint of any sort of censure in his eyes.

'You have a good day, now.' And he swung and strode back to the other car which would take him to work.

Tara closed the door and leant her back against it. Gray couldn't have said anything.

'Why did that man have your car, Auntie Tara? Daisy piped up.

'It's a long story.' And one she had no intention of sharing with her small niece.

Finally, she dropped Daisy off at school and continued on to the salon. She was late — only by ten minutes, but even so, it was unheard of. She always made a point of being in before the other ladies. She maintained it set a good example, and it seemed to work, because they were very rarely late themselves.

They all glanced up from what they were doing as she walked in. Annie, of course, was the first to pass comment.

'Wow! Good night then?'

'Moderately.'

'Hmmm. If you say so.' Annie studied

her for a second or two. 'Gray Madison phoned — um, about two minutes ago, asking to speak to you.'

Tara swallowed nervously. So he'd concluded his breakfast meeting, then. It must have been an extremely brief one. Couldn't wait to use the hatchet on her, no doubt. At least she was expecting it after her behaviour the previous evening. He certainly picked his moment, though. Surely he could have left it a couple of days. As it was, she was feeling extremely vulnerable, and her head was still hammering painfully inside her skull.

'He said,' Annie went on, still watching her intently, 'would you ring him back. His number's on the pad on the desk.'

Tara walked across to the reception desk, and sure enough, there it was — a mobile number. Oh well, best to get it over with. If it was the immediate sack, she'd almost be thankful. It would mean she could go home to bed and stay there, nursing her hangover for the rest of the day.

She tapped in the numbers written on the pad. Gray Madison answered immediately. 'Good morning.'

For a second time, Tara swallowed. 'I-It's Tara, Tara Wyndham. You rang me?' Even she could hear the quiver in her voice, so he surely would.

'Yes, I did. Thanks for ringing back.'

He didn't sound disappointed, or prepared to use his hatchet on her. In fact, if anything, he sounded pleased to hear from her.

'Thank you for getting my car back to me. I hope it wasn't too much trouble.'

'None at all. It was my pleasure. Better to be safe than sorry.'

'Yes, indeed, but still — thank you.' She thought it best to leave the matter there. She didn't want to push her luck. 'Um, how can I help you?' He'd probably checked the February figures and found them wanting. She waited for the inevitable response — *I'm sorry to tell you* . . .

However, it didn't come. In fact,

there was a full moment's silence before he said, 'I've been wondering — would you come out for a meal with me?'

Shocked to the core by the request, Tara pulled the phone away from her face and stared at it in dismay. Clearly he wanted to sack her face to face. But he wouldn't ask her out for a meal to do that, would he? He'd simply summon her to the Birmingham office.

'Tara? Are you still there?'

'Y-yes. Yes. When?' She chewed at her bottom lip. God, she sounded like an idiot. Couldn't she have done better than a blunt 'When?'

'Tomorrow night? I'm free then if you are.'

Quite unable to come up with any sort of credible reason not to agree, as much as she would have liked to, Tara answered, 'Um — well, I'll have to organise a babysitter, but all being well, yes, okay.' She closed her eyes in dismay at what she'd just so rashly consented to. An evening out with Gray Madison — just the two of them? What on earth would they talk about? How many employees was he planning to sack?

But her eyes instantly snapped open again when he asked, 'Your brother still not around then?' He paused just long enough for her to say no before going on, 'If a sitter is a problem, I could probably help out on that score.'

Once again, she regarded the phone — this time incredulously. He sounded unbelievably keen to have her meet him. Why? As she'd initially thought — did he like sacking employees face to face? Did it give him some sort of thrill; the thrill of exerting his power over them?

'My niece is always looking for ways to earn some extra pocket money. She's sixteen, so it would be legal. She's a very sensible, responsible girl.'

'Oh, I don't think that will be necessary, but thank you anyway. I have a friend who's always ready to step in.'

'Okay, if you're sure. Ring me if there's a problem. I'll pick you up at seven thirty, if that's okay?'

'That's fine. Where will we be going? Just so I know what to wear.' Oh good Lord, how pathetic did that sound? This was getting worse and worse. Maybe she should simply refuse to meet him. But after agreeing, it would only make her sound even more pathetic to backtrack now. No, she'd agreed to go, so that was what she'd do.

'Grimaldi's. They know me there, and the food's always excellent.'

Grimaldi's? Where the hell was that? She was none the wiser as to what to wear. Her stomach somersaulted with nerves.

'Where's that? I don't think I know it.'

'On the outskirts of Birmingham. Between there and Harborne.'

'Oh. So casual smart?'

'Smart casual, I suppose is the best description, but really, you don't need to worry. Wear whatever you want. I'm sure you'll look perfect.'

Huh. She wished she was that confident.

She ended the call, ignoring Annie's curious stare, and dialled Bel's number. If she'd ever needed her best friend, it was now. She had to talk to someone about Ricky. She'd burst if she didn't share her fears about his wellbeing with someone. And who better than Bel? But she also wanted — no, needed — to talk about Gray Madison, and get her take on that. Because why on earth he'd ask her out if he was about to sack her, she couldn't imagine. Unless he thought it would soften the blow.

'Bel? It's me, Tara. I need to talk — in complete confidence. You're the only one I can do that with. Can you come round this evening for a drink?'

'I'm intrigued, but yes, of course. I don't seem to have seen you properly for a while — not for a good old natter.'

So Bel would come to the house at eight o'clock. Tara instantly felt calmer. Bel could be a bit of a scatterbrain at times, but she undoubtedly had the knack of putting things into perspective for Tara.

The rest of the day passed quickly and busily, thankfully. Annie had naturally quizzed Tara about Gray's call.

She softly told her, 'He wants to meet me tomorrow evening.'

Annie's eyes widened. 'Really? Business or pleasure?'

Tara frowned. 'I'm not actually sure which. He didn't say.'

Annie slanted a dancing gaze at her. 'Maybe he simply fancies you — have you considered that?'

'Hardly.' Although there had been something in his expression as he'd looked at her a couple of times the previous evening that made the suggestion not completely outrageous. 'He must mix with some wealthy and gorgeous women.'

'You're pretty gorgeous too.' Annie raised an eyebrow. 'Don't put yourself down.'

★ ★ ★

Bel arrived on the dot of eight, bearing a bottle of Tara's favourite red wine. Tara had never been gladder to see anyone. 'Come in. I've opened some wine, but thank you for this.' In fact she'd already had a glass, telling herself that she needed something to help her explain Ricky's disappearance to Bel. Bel's opinion of Ricky had never been very high, so his current behaviour would just serve to reinforce that view. She thought, and had had no compunctions in saying so on a couple of occasions, that Ricky lacked any semblance of maturity and parental responsibility.

'Pour me a very large glass, please. I've never needed an input of alcohol more,' Bel cried. 'I've had a hell of a day. But hey, enough of that — it's you who needs to talk.' She took the glass that Tara was holding out to her, at the same time subjecting her friend to a particularly penetrating stare. 'So shoot. What's wrong? Because I can see something is.'

Tara told her. First of all, about

Ricky's sudden disappearance, and her suspicions about the reason for that. 'He's taken something he shouldn't have. God knows what, and God knows where he is. But I think he's in hiding. He's been gone for eleven days now. I don't know what to do, Bel.'

'And he hasn't been in touch at all?'

'No, not a word. His phone seems to be turned off permanently.' She went on to tell her friend about the mystery caller and the fact that she now suspected he, or someone else, was watching the house.

'Checking to see if Ricky's back, is my guess.' Bel eyed Tara. 'He hasn't actually threatened you, has he?'

'No, not in so many words. But he did say if he doesn't get back whatever it is Ricky's taken — stolen — of his, he'll take something precious of Ricky's.'

'What does that mean? What does Ricky have that's valuable?'

'Nothing that I can think of,' Tara miserably replied. 'But the house and salon have both been broken into.

131

Nothing's missing, so he's obviously searching for whatever it is of his Ricky's taken.'

'You've rung the police, of course?'

'Well, I did that a couple of days after he disappeared, but they weren't interested. Their view was he's a grown man.' She shrugged. 'What if Ricky's actually stolen something really valuable? Say, a lot of money? If I report him missing again after twelve days, they're bound to ask a lot of questions, start an investigation even; and if they find him, he could be arrested.'

'My God.' Bel looked stunned; disbelieving. 'But they'd have to locate this other man first, and he's beginning to sound like some sort of criminal.'

'I know. It's a mess. And just to top it all, Gray Madison has asked me out tomorrow evening for a meal.'

Bel was beginning to look shell shocked. 'Wow. Gray Madison? Your boss? The good-looking one; the one who gave the drinks party?'

Tara nodded.

'Well, it's all happening to you, isn't it? But . . . ' Bel frowned. 'What's the problem with that? He probably wants to discuss business.'

'Or sack me?'

'Why would he do that? And over a meal, to boot?'

'Well, because the fact is, the last four or five months haven't been altogether brilliant for the salon. Takings are very up and down, with rather more down than up, although things are gradually improving. But what's really worrying me is the fact that he's gained a reputation as a bit of a hatchet man.' She pulled a guilty face. 'And I made a bit of a fool of myself at his party. I drank too much and had to ask him to call a taxi for me. He had to get a couple of his employees to bring my car back this morning. So, put it all together and there's a very good case for sacking me.'

'Yes, but still — why would he have invited you to his house if he planned to sack you over your lacklustre profit

figures? Even taking into account your — '
She grinned broadly. ' — drunken behaviour at his party?'

'It wasn't that bad.' But then images of her stumbling and him holding her up passed before her eyes. Oh God, yes, it was. 'And he's seen the past month's figures since then, and although they weren't terrible, they weren't that good either.'

Bel eyed her, head cocked. 'Even, so I can't believe he'd sack you while having a meal at a restaurant. You can't do that anymore at a moment's notice. Employees have to be given a series of warnings.' Her eyes narrowed. 'Where's he taking you?'

'Grimaldi's.'

'That doesn't sound like a venue for a business meeting. It's very, very upmarket, with prices to match.'

'Is it?'

'Mind you, from what I've heard, he won't miss the odd hundred pounds or two.'

'That doesn't reassure me, Bel. He

could only have made so much money by being totally ruthless.'

The remainder of the evening was spent rehashing things and getting nowhere. Bel tried to be supportive, but not even she could reassure Tara this time. In the end, it was eleven thirty before she got up to go.

'Look, things will work themselves out. Gray Madison would've sacked you by now if he was going to. And as for Ricky, I'm sure he'll swan back in full of apologies and with some sort of smooth excuse. He wouldn't leave Daisy just like that. Not even Ricky would be capable of that.' Although her wry expression didn't exactly bear that sentiment out. 'And as for the man who's watching the house and demanding his stuff back, whatever it is, that'll all be a storm in a teacup too; I'd put money on it. Because when all's said and done, what's he going to do? Kidnap you? Hold you for ransom? Till Ricky coughs up? Unlikely.'

But Tara was nowhere near as sure of

any of that as Bel seemed. As for not deserting Daisy — well, Ricky had never really bonded with his small daughter. He'd been a selfish boy and now he was a selfish man. And as much as she loved him, she couldn't deny that fact. But was that her fault? In an effort to compensate for losing his parents at a relatively young age, she had tended to give in to his demands. Could his behaviour now be a direct result of that overindulgence?

She walked Bel to the door and opened it. 'Thanks for coming. You've been just what I needed.'

'No prob. I'm just sorry I couldn't be more help.' She stepped outside and looked around. 'Hey, there's a car parked opposite. You don't think — ?'

With a sense of dread, Tara leant forward. 'It's the same car, I'm sure of it.'

Even as she spoke the words, the vehicle moved off, engine roaring as the driver pressed hard on the accelerator and disappeared down the road.

Bel looked back at Tara, her anxiety plain to see. 'Tara, you really should ring the police. He could be dangerous.' She belatedly looked as troubled as Tara felt.

'I can't.' She wished people would stop saying that. 'What if it gets Ricky into trouble? Oh God,' she moaned, 'if only he'd ring me. I don't know what to do.'

She walked back into the sitting room once Bel had finally left, her head throbbing with worry. She was clearing away the glasses and the empty bottle when the land phone rang.

She froze. It was almost midnight. Who would ring now? Could it be Ricky? Tentatively, she lifted the receiver and placed it against her ear.

'Have you heard from him?' a man's voice growled.

'N-no.' She didn't need to ask who he was talking about. She knew. It was Ricky.

'Are you sure? Because if you're lying — '

'I'm not. Was it you who broke into my home and salon?'

'It might have been.'

'What are you looking for?'

He didn't answer.

'Well, whatever it is, I don't have it. Please leave me alone.'

'If I don't get my goods back, Ricky will pay. You tell him that.'

'I don't know where he is!' she yelled.

'I don't believe you. He wouldn't leave Daisy. Such a pretty little girl. So you tell him. I want what's mine, and if I don't get it, he'll be sorry — as you will be, too.'

7

Tara's heartbeat raced as realisation dawned. He knew; he knew all about Daisy. Her name, what she looked like. Had Ricky shown him a photograph, or had he seen her somewhere? With Tara, maybe? But how would he have known her? Unless — her breath caught in her throat — it really was him, watching the house. He could have seen them both leaving for school or returning later in the day. But more importantly, what had he meant by his threats? What did he plan to do if he didn't get back whatever it was he wanted?

And where the hell was Ricky? This was all his fault. Maybe she *should* ring the police. But what if that landed Ricky in trouble; serious trouble? Jail-time trouble?

Despite the lateness of the hour, she tried his mobile number for the umpteenth time, but all she heard yet again was the electronic voice informing her that her call couldn't be taken and would she leave a message.

Did he not realise the trouble, the heartache, the fear he was causing by his sudden disappearance? Even so, she couldn't bring herself to ring the police.

She didn't sleep that night for agonising over it all. Mainly, what the anonymous caller had meant. What would she be sorry about? He wouldn't hurt her, would he? Fear — well, terror, actually, gripped her.

Not until dawn was breaking did sleep overtake her; and then, of course, she slept through the alarm. By the time she did wake, it was eight thirty. Oh no — even as she had the thought, her door opened and Daisy skipped in.

'I'm all dressed. Why are you still in bed, Auntie Tara? Can't you wake up? We're going to be so-o late.'

Tara sat up. Her head was throbbing and her mouth felt achingly dry. Why, oh why had she drunk all that wine last night? That made it two nights in a row.

She was in grave danger of turning into a lush. She clambered from bed somewhat shakily, her head spinning now as well as throbbing painfully and remorselessly.

How was she going to get through the day? And not only that, there was her date with Gray this evening. Could she cancel? Did she dare? No, she didn't. If her job was on the line, she couldn't risk antagonising him. But apart from that, she didn't want him deciding she was unreliable. It was the very last quality he'd be wanting to discover in a manager.

Eventually she gathered herself together, and in the end they were only ten minutes late for school.

'I don't know what Miss Taylor is going to say,' Daisy sternly admonished Tara.

'Tell her it's all my fault.'

'Hmm.' Daisy ran across the playground into the red brick building.

As for Tara, she headed for the salon. The ladies would be wondering where she was, Annie especially. Fortunately she didn't have any appointments until ten thirty, and then it was just the one. The only heartening thing about that was that no one would be inconvenienced.

She walked in to a chorus of 'Where have you been?'

'I was delayed at home.' Which wasn't a lie — she had been; she hadn't woken up.

'Daisy playing up?' Annie asked.

'No, things just went wrong.' She refused to blame her niece, not when she'd got up and dressed herself. It would have felt like the worst sort of betrayal. She strode directly into the back room and made herself another coffee. Anything to try and ease the turmoil within her.

* * *

By the end of the day, Tara's frame of mind had been restored to normal — well, more or less. The prospect of going out with Gray Madison was still an intimidating one, mainly because she didn't know what to expect from him.

She drove straight home, not having to collect Daisy. Lizzie had rung her and said she'd keep her for the night and, as it was Saturday the next day, she could collect Daisy on the way home from work as usual. Daisy could borrow some of Gemma's night things as well as play clothes for the day.

'It means you won't have to rush home if you're — um, enjoying yourself with Gray.' The last remark was loaded with a great deal of humour and even more innuendo.

Tara ignored it. 'Thanks, Lizzie. I'm really grateful.'

But was she? She had no excuse now to end the evening early if she decided she needed to.

Putting it all from her mind, she concentrated on getting herself ready, her first decision being what to wear. Oh Lord, she wearily thought, she still hadn't purchased anything new; and once again, nothing she owned seemed remotely suitable for a venue like Grimaldi's. The trouble was, she never seemed to have the time to go shopping.

In the end, she plumped for a dress — again. She only owned two, one of which she'd already worn to Gray's drinks party, so she couldn't wear that. The trouble was, they were both four or five years old. Still, each was in a fairly classical style, and so hadn't dated. That only left her one alternative: a black slim-fitting dress with a deep boat neckline and a skirt which gently flared at the bottom and ended just above her knees. It was a flattering style, though just like the other one, it clung a bit too snugly to her figure. She twirled in front of the mirror. She had definitely put on weight; her breasts were fuller, and so several inches of creamy flesh were visible once more above the neckline. Depressingly, once again, she had to resort to chunky beads to conceal what she could of all that was on display. A diet was definitely called for. She'd start tomorrow.

She finally slipped a jacket on and went downstairs to await Gray's arrival, which turned out to be within a couple of minutes. Upon hearing the deep-throated sound of a vehicle's engine, she went into the kitchen to look out of the window. He was in the red Ferrari. She chewed at her bottom lip. How on earth was she going to climb into that without exposing several inches of thigh?

As Gray, with enviable ease, climbed from the driver's seat, she hurried back into the hallway. She didn't want him to catch her watching him; he was far too self-assured already. She glanced into the mirror on the wall of the hall, rearranged the beads to conceal the maximum that she could, and then tweaked a couple of strands of hair back into place before opening the front door.

'Good evening.' He smiled at her. 'Ready? Ye-es, I can see you are.' His gaze roamed over her from her head to her toes.

Don't I look it? she was tempted to ask. However, she thought better of it. 'Y-yes.'

She pulled the door closed behind her and prepared herself mentally for what could turn out to be a very difficult evening ahead. And the first hurdle to overcome was that of climbing into the low-slung vehicle without completely demolishing her modesty. She was gratified, therefore, to successfully achieve that ambition, apart from the briefest flash of thigh. To her relief, Gray didn't seem to notice, although she detected a disturbing gleam to his eye as he took his own seat once more.

They didn't talk much on the way to the restaurant, other than for polite pleasantries. All Tara could think then was what on earth they would talk about for the rest of the evening. What could they possibly have in common, apart from her management of That Special Touch? And, with the best will in the world, that conversation wouldn't last for much more than fifteen minutes. How much could you say about disappointing profit margins?

However, once they reached the

extremely elegant and sophisticated Grimaldi's and had been shown to their table by the formally attired maître d', things took a more encouraging turn.

Gray ordered a bottle of red wine — a very expensive bottle, Tara guessed, judging by the antiquity of the label; it was starting to peel off. A waiter handed them a menu each, at the same time indicating with a warm smile and the murmured words, 'And how are you this evening, Mr Madison?' that he knew Gray well, which led Tara to wonder how many other women he'd brought here. She wouldn't mind betting they'd been a damn sight more glamorous and beautiful than her — and they certainly wouldn't have been attired in a five-year-old dress that was too tight and way too revealing.

Gray lifted his glass in a smiling salute to her and said, 'Here's to us,' which did rather confuse her. What the hell did that mean? There was no 'us'. Maybe he was referring to their business relationship? Because she couldn't believe he'd think there'd ever be anything more meaningful between them. They inhabited very different worlds, as she'd decided once before. His an extremely privileged one; hers — well, suffice it to say, considerably less well privileged.

However, she did respond by lifting her own glass and weakly smiling before taking a large mouthful of her wine. She was so nervous by this time that she needed some sort of fortification. However, it made no difference; her fingers were trembling, she noticed.

'Relax,' Gray murmured.

She widened her eyes at him. Was her apprehension so noticeable? But surprisingly, it was he who took a steadying breath. So he wasn't quite as calm as he made out. That, in a strange way, reassured her. It indicated that he was human, after all.

However, if it had been nervousness that had afflicted him — and she couldn't really believe it was — it didn't last long, because he went on to say with enviable confidence, 'Tell me about yourself.'

Once again, she stared at him. This was beginning to sound alarmingly like a real date. She'd been expecting him to get straight down to business, discussing ways and means of improving the salon's turnover — even if it only took fifteen minutes. Instead of which . . . She took a deep breath, which was a mistake, because she felt the fabric of her bodice straining as her breasts swelled beneath it, in all likelihood revealing even more naked flesh to him. Good grief, she hoped he didn't think she was doing it deliberately in order to — well, try and seduce him.

However, Gray didn't seem to notice. All he did was mutter something that sounded remarkably like, 'And will you stop looking at me like that — please.'

She must have misheard. But something was affecting him physically. His face had paled and his eyes darkened beneath their hooded lids. However, despite his reaction to — whatever — he held her gaze with his, minute flecks appearing in his amber eyes as he did so. This had the effect of turning them almost gold, which along with the thick, dark blond hair, one lock of which persisted in dropping over his forehead, made him appear — the only appropriate word she could come up with was leonine. She half expected him to give a growl and toss his mane.

Bemused by all of this, she asked, 'What do you want to know?'

'All about you. Everything.'

The bluntness of his demand startled her, but somehow she managed to respond evenly and steadily. 'Well, I'm not married. As I've already told you, I have a younger brother, Ricky, who has a daughter, Daisy. She's five. I look after her.'

She paused, allowing him the opportunity to say, 'Her mother doesn't seem to figure in all of this. What's happened to her?'

Tara shrugged. 'Haven't a clue. She disappeared a couple of days after she'd given birth. She and Ricky were very young, and they weren't married. She simply — went.'

Gray's brow lowered into a frown. 'So how do you manage, raising a child and running the salon?'

Tara expected him to say 'No wonder you aren't making much of a success of it', but he didn't. She held her breath. Would this be the excuse he needed to get rid of her? How stupid of her, to be so heedlessly frank. She had to rectify this straight away; reassure him that she could manage both, and had been managing both for five years.

'Well, she started school last September, and a friend collects her after school and looks after her till I leave work. I pick her up on the way home.' Her voice trailed off. His frown had deepened. Had she just talked herself out of a job?

'And your brother — where's he while all this is going on?'

Tara shrugged. 'Well, he does what he can.'

'He works, presumably?'

She nodded.

151

'What does he do?'

'A bit of this, a bit of that.'

The truth was Ricky had never been able to stick at anything, not even as a boy at school. He'd have mad crazes. One had been that he was going to be a scientist of some sort, before just as suddenly he'd changed tack and declared he was going to be an engineer. Then that too had vanished just as rapidly. His various jobs, once he'd left school, had never lasted for more than a couple of months, when he'd announce he was bored with that, couldn't see a future in it, and off he'd go on yet another fruitless tangent. That was when he'd sometimes disappear for a few days — recharging his batteries, he'd tell her when he returned. But he'd always come back then, not like now.

And as for his friends, the least said about them the better. Not that Tara knew many of them. The few she had met hadn't inspired any confidence in her that they would be a beneficial influence upon Ricky. But this time, this absence was lasting longer than ever before. It was also much more disturbing; not least because of the recurring appearances and phone calls of the mystery man. Plus, Ricky had never turned his phone off before. It had always been on, like some sort of physical attachment to him. Could he have simply lost it? That seemed the most plausible explanation. For surely he wouldn't have turned it off? Had this man threatened him, and so he'd got rid of his phone and disappeared to somewhere safe, thus making sure he couldn't be contacted? But why hadn't he told Tara? That was what she didn't understand.

Gray's eyes had narrowed, as if he'd read her racing thoughts.

'So he's not available to babysit his daughter?'

She shook her head. 'Not at the moment, no.'

'Can't your parents help out?'

'They're dead.'

'Oh God, I'm sorry. What happened?'

'A motorway pile-up, nine years ago.'

'So you've brought up your brother and now you're raising his daughter. All on your own, by the sound of it.'

'I don't mind. She's a sweetheart. I love her very much.'

'And the house you're in?' He was still watching her intently.

'It was the family home. I've managed to keep it. My father's life insurance policy took care of the remaining mortgage.'

'You must have been very young at the time. What are you now? Twenty five, six?'

'Thirty, actually. Ricky was fourteen when it happened. I was twenty-one, so I was considered old enough to take responsibility for him, otherwise he would have been taken into care.'

'So I presume you found a sitter for this evening?'

'Yes. Lizzie, who I've already mentioned. She has a daughter, Gemma, the same age as Daisy, so it works well. They're great friends.'

This was beginning to feel more like an interrogation than mere curiosity. Time to give the table a spin, she decided.

'So,' she began, 'enough about me. How about you? Are you married with a family?'

'I was. We divorced four years ago, but I have a son, Daniel. He's nine. He lives with his mother, Marisa, but he spends most of his holidays with me.'

'Oh, I see.'

He gave a half smile and went on, 'To fill in the details. I'm thirty-seven years old. We married far too young. I was twenty-three, Marisa was twenty-one. It was fine to start with, but then we had Daniel. She felt tied down; she'd always enjoyed a hectic social life. We tried to make it work, for Daniel's sake, but it was a hopeless task, and she . . . well, she met someone else.' He shrugged. 'The only answer was divorce. We're both happier now, and it doesn't seem to have detrimentally affected Daniel either. I bought Osborne House, as you know, a few months ago. I'm intending to make some changes. It needs quite extensive restoration in certain parts.

'My parents live in Oxford, so I see quite a bit of them. I have one sister, Vanessa, married to Sam, and a sixteen-year-old niece, Sara. I mentioned her as a possible sitter for Daisy. She's growing up far too quickly.' He gave a rueful smile. 'And that's about it, I think.'

'What do you do, apart from the salons? Oh, and I heard you also have a chain of DIY stores, Homes and Gardens?'

'Yes, that's right. They're just about everywhere, too. There's one outside of Worcester. I like to think they're a bit more upmarket than the average. I'm also moving into the development of AI, Artificial Intelligence. It's early days for me, but it's going to be huge and it's happening fast. I intend to be in the game when it really takes off in the UK. I play the financial markets — reasonably successfully.' He gave a modest smile. 'I'm also in the process of developing my own line in the high-end clothing business, for men and women. I've found a designer, and I'm presently setting up the production side of it. If all goes well, I'm planning on opening a couple of stores in the southeast within the next twelve to eighteen months. I want to see how the clothes sell before investing in a chain of stores.'

'Wow! It must all keep you very busy. I'm surprised you moved out of the southeast with all this going on.'

'I was tired of the rat race there. And I can run things from here, no problem. I employ some excellent people who are in charge in the various locations, so I don't need to be there.'

Which sounded the exact opposite of what his partner had told her. That Gray was a hands-on person.

'And I like to make time for other things when I can.'

Other things being women, Tara assumed. The waiter appeared at their table. 'Can I take your orders?'

'Oh, um . . . ' Tara glanced at the menu. 'I'll have the Salad Niçoise and the grilled salmon, please.'

Gray regarded her. 'Would you like more time?'

'No, thank you. That will be fine.'

He said no more and proceeded to study the menu before saying, 'I'll have the same, please.'

Once the waiter had left, an uncomfortable silence descended on them.

'You must be wondering why I've asked you for a meal,' Gray finally said.

'To give me the sack?' she quipped.

He stared at her, his brow lowered into a frown. 'Is that what you've been thinking?'

'Well, I can't think of any other reason.'

'Can't you?' The gold flecks that she'd glimpsed a couple of times now appeared in his eyes.

'N-no.'

He continued to scrutinise her before saying, 'You haven't considered the fact that you're a very lovely woman

— beautiful, appealing, smart?'

She met his gaze uncertainly now. 'Not really, no.'

He didn't speak for several seconds. 'Do you have so little confidence in yourself?' He raised an eyebrow.

She didn't answer, not because she couldn't, but because she genuinely didn't know what to say to that.

'I asked you out because I'd like to get to know you — and not just as the manager of one of my salons.'

Still Tara couldn't find any words. She was completely confused. This man must have women flocking around him, so why waste his time on her?

A smile tilted his lips as he watched her struggle to comprehend his intent. 'The truth is, I find you immensely appealing and I'd like to see more of you.' He lowered his voice. 'Much more.' The final two words were seductively throaty.

Tara felt the beginnings of a blush warming her face. And still she couldn't speak, other than to say, 'Oh?' For

God's sake, how stupid she must sound. Infantile, even. And even more humiliating, he thought she'd deliberately displayed her wares for him to see. Or, at least, that was what she took his last words to mean.

'Oh? Is that it? Oh?' A smile flirted with the corners of his mouth.

'Well, y-you must have lots of women interested in you. Women much more lovely, beautiful even, than me.'

'Well, I suppose that's true. I've taken out quite a few over the years.'

Her breast swelled in indignation. Did he have to agree?

'But.' He cocked his head, his eyes narrowing as they roamed slowly over her, lingering deliberately, it seemed to Tara, on the voluptuous flesh being displayed for his appraisal. 'You have something else.'

Yes, she thought, bigger breasts, something a good few of these designer-clad women didn't have. In fact, some of them resembled stick insects rather than having a normal womanly shape. God knew what they ate. A couple of lettuce leaves a week, probably.

'Something more than mere beauty. There's an innocence about you, a natural warmth, and . . . honesty, I suppose. You say what you think.' He grinned at her now. 'You also have spectacularly beautiful eyes. They're what, hazel? Light brown flecked with green and gold. And your figure.' Again his gaze roamed over what he could see of her above the top of the table. 'You're lovely, Tara. Perfect, in fact.' His gaze returned to her distinctly and uncomfortably flushed face. 'I want to go on seeing you. Get to really know you.'

Luckily, the waiter appeared with their starters at that point, so Tara didn't have to say anything. Which was just as well, because she had absolutely no idea how to respond to all he'd just said. She'd never had a man like Gray so unashamedly admiring of her, and expressing it in no uncertain terms, moreover. He was like no one she'd ever known.

As if he sensed her discomfort, Gray changed the subject. 'So what do you do for relaxation?'

And their conversation took another turn altogether. They discussed their favourite writers — both of them were keen readers — their favourite foods, television programmes, choice of music; and suddenly it was eleven o'clock, and with their desserts eaten and coffee drunk, it was time to leave.

All of Tara's uncertainties returned in a torrent. What would Gray be expecting of her? To make love? After all, the meal in its entirety must have cost a fortune. Would he want something in return? She'd been out with men who'd made no secret of the fact that they'd expected exactly that, and more than one of them had turned scarily nasty when she'd demurred and rejected their romantic advances. She recalled one case in particular. She'd been just twenty-three. Ben Hudson had been his name. He'd seemed perfectly amenable all evening; had talked easily and knowledgably about all sorts of things. She'd even found herself thinking, *I could really get on with this man.* Then at the end of the date, she'd assumed he was driving her straight home, but instead he had taken her to a secluded spot a mile or so outside of the town, where she'd pretty quickly found herself literally fighting him off. She'd managed to climb from the car, to the accompaniment of his shouted 'Okay, you frigid bitch, you can walk home. I didn't spend all that money just to be refused.' And that was what she had to do. It had been a cold winter's night and she hadn't been dressed appropriately, but somehow she'd managed it, despite her three-inch heels.

It had stopped her dating for a considerable time afterwards, practically destroying her trust in men, all men. Even now, she carefully decided just who she'd meet, and there weren't very many. In any case, going out on dates nowadays wasn't so easy with

Daisy to care for. It did, though, provide her with a very convenient excuse if she really didn't want to meet someone.

However, upon their return to her house, Gray parked the car and, after turning off the ignition, climbed from the driver's seat and walked round to help her out. Well, to be truthful, he grasped both of her hands and literally hauled her out. She was feeling decidedly intoxicated, but even so, her nerves began jangling again. It was decision time. Should she invite him in or not? And if she did, would he interpret that as an invitation to make love? She rather thought he might, considering the way he'd looked at her at one point in the evening.

But he made the decision for her. Taking her by the elbow, he steered her to her front door.

'Do you have your keys?' he then asked.

She rummaged in her bag and finally located them, nestled in the very

164

bottom. She handed them to him, and he unlocked the door. He then simply stood there, making no move to enter. Tara stared at him, suddenly torn by a deep longing to feel his arms about her, his mouth on hers.

Decision made.

'D-do you want to come in — for a coffee, or . . . ?'

He didn't immediately answer, but simply looked back at her, his head cocked to one side. 'Better not.' The words were low and throaty, his eyes dark and glittering at her from beneath hooded lids.

Tara took a deep breath and said, 'Okay.' She hoped her disappointment didn't reveal itself. Did he not want her? Yet his remarks earlier about wanting to see more of her, much more, had seemed to suggest the exact opposite. She wrinkled her brow in confusion.

Something glinted in his eye then, but all he said was, 'I'll wish you good night and say how much I've enjoyed this evening. We must do it again. I'll call you.' And with that, he spun around and strode to his car.

Tara watched him drive off, her frustration at what felt very much like an anti-climax engulfing her.

8

She dreamt about Gray that night. He'd come into the house with her and taken her into his arms, kissing her passionately, expertly, tenderly, his hands caressing her — but disappointingly, the dream ended there.

She awoke before the alarm went off, still racked with frustrated longings. The majority of men would have accepted her invitation and proceeded to make love to her. But Gray Madison, she was beginning to realise, was unlike any other man she'd ever met. By look and word, he'd led her to believe he wanted to make love to her and then ultimately declined her invitation. Had that been deliberate provocation; a desire to tease her? But he hadn't seemed the type to tease. Or had he known it would intrigue her? Make her want him, by forcing her to wait for him? Yes, that seemed much more likely. Clever tactics. He'd be accustomed to using such methods in his business dealings. And he liked to win. That had been made very evident to her. Well, she'd leave the ball in his hands. She could also play the waiting game.

She sailed through work that day, despite spending the whole time waiting for Gray's phone call. When it didn't come, she again found herself wondering if he'd merely been toying with her, after all. Or had he decided she wasn't really his type? She had hinted at that, after all. Maybe he'd secretly agreed with her. But when she recalled the glint in his eye as they'd said good night, that seemed unlikely. The truth was, she didn't know what to make of him. He was proving an enigma; unreadable, inscrutable, maddening. She sighed. That could be intentional, as well.

Such was her uncertainty about him that when Mark Bellamy rang to ask her out that evening, she agreed. She was sorely in need of a distraction. She was sure Lizzie wouldn't mind keeping Daisy until Sunday morning. Gemma loved having her there, and Lizzie often said her life was much easier when Daisy stayed. And sure enough, when she phoned her, her friend immediately agreed.

'Are you sure, Lizzie? I don't want to impose.'

'Don't be silly, you're not. She and Gemma play so well together, I actually get some time to myself.'

She and Mark had arranged to meet at The Bistro, the only decent restaurant in Mallow End. There was a hamburger place, but that was mostly frequented by teenagers who didn't seem to mind their words being drowned out by loud rock music.

'I can pick you up if you'd rather,' Mark said.

But Tara preferred to drive herself. That way, she could leave if things didn't work out and also avoid any of the unpleasantness she'd experienced in the past when he delivered her home again.

They'd agreed to meet at eight o'clock, so Tara left home at ten to. It was sometimes difficult to park in the town and she didn't want to have to rush.

In the end there were no spaces left at the kerbside outside of The Bistro, so she had to make do with parking a few minutes' walk away, in a side road. She then had to make a dash for the restaurant, not wanting to be too late. Which meant she was out of breath when she got there.

Mark was already seated at a table for two at the back of the room with a glass of red wine in front of him. He made no attempt to hide his relief at her appearance, immediately getting to his feet to hold the opposite chair out for her to sit down.

'Sorry,' she blurted, 'couldn't park.'

'You should have let me collect you,' he pointed out, clearly irritated by her refusal to allow him to do that.

'It seemed an unnecessary bother when it's such a short drive for me.'

'Well, you're here now.' He smiled at her. 'I've got a bottle of red. I hope that's okay.'

'It's fine. Thank you.' She picked up her glass once he'd filled it and said, 'Cheers.'

'Here's to a great evening,' he replied. 'I must admit I was a little surprised when you agreed to meet me.'

She had no time to respond to that because the waiter arrived to take their order. She wouldn't have known what to say, in any case. Mainly because he was right; she had been reluctant to see him again. Now, she found herself wondering whether she had, in fact, done the right thing. His face seemed even redder than it had the evening of Gray's party, leading her to wonder if he'd already been drinking. She glanced at the wine bottle. It was almost two thirds empty already, so clearly he had. She'd only had a glassful out of it.

Which seemed to indicate that he must have arrived here before the few minutes it had taken her to walk here. She surreptitiously glanced at her watch. She was ten minutes late, and he certainly looked as if he'd been drinking for longer than that. Thank heavens she'd brought her own car. She wouldn't have wanted him to drive her home.

Mark proceeded to take a hefty mouthful of his wine before asking, 'So how've you been?'

'Fine. Busy, of course. I have a niece to take care of as well as a job, as I think I told you on Wednesday.'

'Yes, you did.' He eyed her. 'No trouble getting a babysitter, then? Or is her father taking care of her?'

'No, I asked a friend.' It was her turn now to take a large mouthful of wine.

He leant back in his chair and narrowed his eyes at her. 'Her father still not around?'

'No.'

'Where is he?'

'Away on business.'

'I thought you'd said he had a habit of disappearing?'

Damn. Why had she told him that? The result of too much champagne? She'd take good care to remain sober this evening. She didn't want to repeat her indiscretions of Wednesday evening. The fewer people who knew about Ricky's unreliability, the better. If Gray heard about it, it could place her job in even more jeopardy. Because why would he continue to employ a manager who had troubles at home that could interfere with her work? Stop her coming to work, even? 'Oh, I was exaggerating. I was a bit miffed with him over something, that was all.'

'So you expect him back?'

'Oh, good Lord, yes. Any time now. In fact, he could be home by the time I get back.' *If only*, she reflected, allowing herself another generous mouthful of her wine. She'd always hated any form of deceit, probably because she was no good at it.

173

'Good, good. We can do this again then.' He grinned at her, well pleased with himself, obviously.

'Oh well, I — um, we'll have to see.' And so yet again, she'd got it wrong. She should just have admitted she didn't know when, if ever, her brother would be back. Now she'd have to come up with some other excuse not to meet him.

The waiter brought their meals at that point, to Tara's heartfelt relief. She shouldn't have agreed to meet him. Her initial instinct had been the right one.

The conversation after that became slightly stilted, and Tara quickly realised she had nothing whatsoever in common with Mark Bellamy. What made the entire thing even more strained was the fact that he emptied the wine bottle and instantly ordered another.

'Oh,' Tara began, 'no more for me Mark, thank you. I have to drive.'

'No worries. You can always leave your car and I'll take you.'

'But you've already had more — '

However, she stopped talking abruptly beneath his outraged stare.

'I'm fine, I can assure you. Certainly capable of driving you home.' But he waved the waiter over and cancelled the second bottle.

Tara carried on eating the fish she'd ordered. But the silence between them was beginning to feel so uncomfortable, she was driven to ask, 'Tell me about your day?' This was despite her reluctance to be compelled to listen to more of the same sort of anecdote she'd had to suffer at Gray's party.

To her surprise, all he said was, 'Oh, nothing out of the ordinary. Pretty boring, as a matter of fact.' He wrapped his fingers around the stem of his glass and asked, 'Where did you disappear to on Wednesday? One minute you were there, the next you'd gone.'

'I took a taxi home. The champagne had gone to my head just a little.'

'But you only had a couple of glasses, didn't you?' he scoffed, before going on to ask, 'What did you make of Gray

Madison? It was the first time you'd met him, wasn't it?'

'No, the second. He seemed . . . ' She shrugged. 'Okay.' She decided not to mention their meal together the evening before. The mood that Mark was swiftly descending into was an increasingly belligerent one; even his colour was deepening. She wasn't sure how he'd react to that news.

'Well.' He gave a snort of scorn. 'He seemed to like you.'

'Really? I didn't notice.'

'All I'll say is, watch yourself with him. He likes the ladies a bit too much.'

'Funny, that,' she drawled. 'He said the same thing about you.'

Tara was beginning to feel distinctly uneasy. She prayed he wasn't going to end up drunk. That was the last thing she needed. She hardly ever went out in the evening, and when she did, she ended up with a man who clearly made a habit of drinking too much, judging by his florid complexion.

'Did he? Damned cheek.'

Anger heightened the colour his face even further. Why the hell had she told him that? It could be the trigger for even more unpleasantness.

'Talk about the kettle calling the pot black.' His lip curled with derision. 'I can promise you, you'll be perfectly safe with me. I like you, Tara.' He leant forward towards her, trying to clasp one of her hands. She tried to slide it out of his reach, but he simply leant further forward and grasped it. She only just stopped herself from shuddering with distaste. His hand was clammy. 'I hope I can see you again.'

'Well, I don't.'

She stopped talking as her gaze reached over his shoulder, her eyes widening in horrified embarrassment. Because who should be walking through the door but Gray, accompanied by his business partner, Cameron.

She glanced back at Mark. It was more than evident he'd had too much to drink. What on earth was Gray going to think? And here she was, holding his hand. Oh God. She wanted nothing more in that second than to crawl under the table. Anything to prevent Gray from spotting her with the very man he'd warned her against.

But then again, he wasn't any better. He'd promised to ring her and hadn't. In which case, she could meet any man she chose to. It just wouldn't be Mark again.

But her fear was instantly realised. Because Gray's face as he saw her and Mark darkened with displeasure. She saw him mutter something to Cameron right before he headed towards her and Mark.

'Well, well,' Mark murmured, 'talk of the devil and he'll surely appear.'

'Bellamy,' Gray curtly said before turning his gaze upon Tara. 'I didn't expect to see you here together.' His gaze took in the clasped hands as his lips compressed with clear distaste. It was transparently obvious that Mark had had too much to drink. Especially when he struggled to his feet, swaying as he said, 'Madison.'

Tara was incapable of saying anything, so it was up to Mark to demand, 'Why didn't you? We g-got on so well at your party, we thought we'd carry on where we left it. Isn't that so, Tara?'

Tara heard herself stammer, 'Um — we-ell, I-I suppose so.'

'Really? Are you okay?' Gray glanced back at Mark, his concern plain to see. Mark had slumped down into his seat and was draining his wine glass of the last few drops. He turned back to Tara. 'Are you driving yourself?'

'Yes. I've parked nearby.'

'Well,' he murmured, 'I should leave ASAP if I were you.'

She managed a tremulous smile as she murmured, 'I fully intend to.'

'Good. I'll be just across the room. I'll ring you in the morning. You'll be at home — alone, I presume?' He glanced meaningfully at Mark.

'Oh yes — apart from Daisy, that is.'

'And where is Daisy this evening?'

'At Lizzie's still.'

'Right. Well, I need to get back to Cameron. Lots to talk about. You and I will speak in the morning. Okay?'

She nodded. And he was gone, leaving both her Mark staring after him.

'Why is he going to ring you in the morning? Is there something going on between you?'

'Not really. I went for a meal with him last evening.' She briefly closed her eyes in exasperation with herself. Why on earth had she told him that? Right after she'd decided not to. What was wrong with her? Her tongue seemed to have a will of its own these days. Sooner or later, it was going to land her in real trouble. If it hadn't already.

Mark eyes had opened wide and suddenly he looked sober again. 'You did? Why the hell would you do that?'

'I don't think that's any of your business, Mark.'

'Don't you? You're here with me and you calmly inform me you were out with him last night. I think it's everything to do with me.'

'It was simply a meal.'

'In which case it begs the question, why is he going to ring you in the morning?'

'I don't know. Maybe there's something he wishes to discuss with me. Business. I do work for him.'

'I know that. But business?' He snorted his incredulity. 'If you believe it's just that, then you're a fool. He wants a damn sight more than to talk business. That was more than obvious, just from the way he looked at you. Well, I can't compete with the great and mighty Gray Madison, so there's no point in prolonging this — date, if you can call it that. You quite clearly don't want to be here with me. So have you finished?' He indicated her empty plate.'

'I have — yes, thank you.'

'Right. I'll get the bill and we'll go.' He clicked his fingers at the hovering waiter. 'The bill, please.'

It took her completely by surprise. 'Oh. Right. Um — okay. Well, we'll go halves, of course.'

'No, we won't. I invited you, so I'll pay.'

'Mark, please.' Belatedly, she was aware of Gray staring across at them both. She glanced towards him. He raised his eyebrows in mute question. She smiled reassurance at him.

'Will you stop staring at him?' Mark said through gritted teeth. 'You're with me — me,' he furiously emphasized, and slapped his hand hard against his chest. 'You bloody women. You're all alike.'

'I-I'm sorry.'

'Yeah, I'm sure you are. Ready?' He flung some notes onto the table and stalked towards the door. Tara meekly followed, not wanting to give him any more reason to remonstrate with her, or make a worse scene that he already was. The whole restaurant must be listening to them. Several people were certainly looking their way, some exhibiting curiosity; others, amusement. She slanted a glance at Gray and noted his anxious expression. She lifted a hand in farewell and followed Mark outside.

'Where's your car?' he demanded to know. 'I'll walk you back.'

'There's no need. As I said, it's nearby.'

'I'm not letting you walk alone. I wouldn't put it past Madison to come after you.'

'I'm sure he won't.'

'I'm coming with you.'

His expression was one of pure fury, and she didn't want to antagonise him any further. Who knew how he'd behave after the display of the last few moments. They walked back to where she'd left her car in silence, Tara making out she didn't notice his increasingly unsteady gait. However, it was with considerable relief that she reached her car. 'Here it is.'

'Right. Well, that's that then. If you should feel inclined to meet again — if things don't go well with Madison, for example . . . ' He smirked at her. ' . . . which knowing his reputation for playing the field, is quite likely, as love 'em and leave 'em is his usual game plan — ring me.'

'I'm sure you're wrong about him.' Tara said.

'Believe me, I'm not.' His eyes were stormy as he regarded her.

'Okay.' She turned to him and said, 'Well, thank you for the meal. I wish you'd let me pay half.'

'Well, if you're determined to repay me, how about a good night kiss? I think I deserve that, at least.' And he reached out for her.

She tried unsuccessfully to evade his clutch. 'No, Mark — please.' She could smell his wine-laden breath, along with a sweaty mustiness. Her stomach heaved in revulsion as he pulled her close and tightened his hold on her. When he bent his head to hers, all Tara could do was to stand absolutely still, hoping her lack of any sort of response would discourage him. It didn't. He ground his mouth brutally over hers, completely oblivious to the fact that she wasn't responding in any way. At last, he lifted his head and stared at her. His mouth twisted into a sneer.

'Bit of a cold fish, aren't you? Does Madison realise that? From what I've heard, he likes his women hot and compliant. Don't think you'll fit the bill somehow.' He was still sneering at her, his eyes two black slits.

'Maybe not, but then I wouldn't know what he likes.' How did she manage to get herself into these situations? Did she never learn?

'Oh.' He grimaced in surprise. 'You didn't get anything from him last evening, then? Doesn't sound like him. You must have repulsed him, too.' He gave another self-satisfied smirk.

'It was just a meal, that's all.'

'Well, don't say I didn't warn you.'

Tara turned and unlocked her car door. 'Good night, Mark, and thanks for the meal.'

'You're welcome. At least now I know you for the frigid bitch you are, and I needn't waste any more time on you.

So contrary to what I said a moment ago, don't ring me when he casts you aside.'

Ignoring that final remark — it really wasn't worthy of any sort of response — Tara climbed into her car, turned on the engine, and pressed her foot hard on the accelerator, making the car leap forward. A swift glance in the driving mirror showed Mark standing still, watching her go.

Well, she reflected, that was one experience she wouldn't be repeating. Lord knew what Gray would have made of it.

★ ★ ★

As Gray had promised, he rang the next morning. She'd already fetched Daisy from Lizzie's and was in the process of ironing her clothes for school.

'It's Gray,' were his first words.

'Hello.'

'How are you?'

'Fine. You?'

'Was everything okay last evening? I almost followed you. I didn't much care for the way Bellamy was behaving.'

'It was fine. I can more than take care of myself.' Huh! If only.

'Only, things seemed to go awry after we spoke; and then when you left so soon afterwards, well — I was concerned. Are you sure you're okay?'

'Yes. We'd finished our meals, so . . . '

'So?'

'No point in staying, really.'

'So, you won't be seeing him again, then?'

'No. Actually, he was a bit miffed when I told him you and I had been out for a meal. That, and too much wine — for him, not me.' She wanted to put him straight on that aspect of it. She didn't want him to think she'd also drunk too much; that it was in any way a habit of hers. The evening of his drinks party had been bad enough. 'Well, let's say it didn't end well.'

These was a tense silence, and then, 'He didn't . . . ?'

She anticipated what he was asking. Did Mark assault her, hurt her in any way? 'No.'

'It was my fault. I shouldn't have mentioned ringing you today. But I wanted him to know you aren't . . . ' His words petered out.

'Know I'm not — what?'

'It doesn't matter.'

She sensed what he'd been about to say, though, even if he wouldn't actually speak the words. That she wasn't free to see Mark anymore. A thrill shot through her at that. Gray Madison was interested in her. Mark had been right about that, at least.

'It's better everything's out in the open,' she said, 'and it's nothing to do with Mark who I see or speak to.'

'Quite. So um, I was wondering . . . '

Tara waited. Could that be nervousness, uncertainty that she could detect in his voice? Surely not.

'Are you and Daisy doing anything today?'

9

Tara didn't hesitate. 'No, we've nothing planned.' She closed her eyes in despair. Now he'd think she'd been waiting on his phone call — which, of course, she had been. She just didn't want him to know that.

'Well, how about we go out, the three of us? If her father wouldn't mind, that is.'

'He's not here,' she blurted. 'What were you thinking of doing?'

'It's a lovely day.'

Tara glanced through the kitchen window. It was. She hadn't noticed till then. The day had been an overcast one when she'd gone to fetch Daisy, but now she could see that the clouds had burned off and the sky was an uninterrupted blue, the sun blazing down. A perfect spring morning, in fact. Even the birds were merrily proclaiming their exuberance, filling the air with their song.

'And I wondered if you fancied a trip out? I have some friends who own a farm in the Cotswolds. They have a pet centre for children. Daisy could actually touch the animals and feed them; it's very safe. What do you think? We could have lunch somewhere on the way.'

'I think I'd like that, and I'm sure Daisy would be ecstatic. Can I just ask her what she thinks?'

'Sure. I'll wait.'

Tara laid the phone down and called, 'Daisy? Could you come here?'

There was no answer. She walked to the bottom of the stairs. 'Daisy?'

'Yes.' The little girl came from her bedroom to stand at the top of the stairs. Her eyes were bright with unshed tears, and her mouth quivered. 'Is it Daddy?'

'No, darling. It's a friend of mine. He wants to know if you'd — we'd like to go out with him for the day. To a farm. What do you think?'

The tears vanished in an instant and Daisy beamed. 'Oh, yes please.' And she practically leapt down the stairs towards her aunt. Tara took her by the hand and returned to pick up her phone again.

'Yes, please, we'd like that.'

'Good. So I'll pick you up in an hour.' It was ten thirty now. 'If that suits you, of course.'

'We'll be ready and waiting.'

It wasn't until Tara had put the phone down once more that she wondered how three of them would fit into Gray's Ferrari. He must have another car, she reasoned. If not, they were going to be in trouble.

She and Daisy were ready in good time, Daisy quivering with anticipation as she waited at the sitting room window for Gray's arrival. She asked at one point, 'What if Daddy comes home and we're not here?'

'I'll leave a note,' Tara quickly said.

That satisfied Daisy, and she turned back to continue her watch at the window. 'Here's a car,' she cried, and ran into the hallway to pull on her jacket.

Tara went to the window and saw Gray climbing out of a metallic grey Range Rover. Just as she'd speculated, he had another vehicle. She followed Daisy to the door, stopping on the way to slip on her own lightweight jacket. For all that it was bright and sunny, it was still only March, and the weather could change in a second.

The doorbell rang and Tara opened it. Gray stood there, dressed in jeans and a shirt. A sweater was draped over his shoulders. As usual, he looked heart-achingly handsome.

Again, she asked herself why a man like this, handsome, rich, with every-thing going for him, should be interested in her. Because the warmth in his amber eyes as he regarded her made it transpar-ently clear that he was.

'Hi, I'm Daisy.' The little girl thrust out a hand to him. 'It's so very nice to meet you.'

Tara watched as Gray made a

superhuman effort to hide his amusement at this charmingly quaint greeting
from a five-year-old. He succeeded
admirably, and leant over until his gaze
was more or less level with hers before
he shook her tiny hand and said, 'It's
very nice to meet you too, Daisy.' He
then glanced up at Tara and asked, 'Are
you ready?'

Again, Daisy took charge. 'Yes, we
are, aren't we, Auntie Tara?'

'Good.' Gray allowed himself a wide
grin now. 'So let's go.'

As they walked out to the car, Daisy
slipped her small hand into Gray's and
proceeded to skip alongside of him.
Gray smiled at Tara and mouthed,
'She's gorgeous.'

Tara smiled back. She couldn't
believe how quickly Daisy had accepted
and taken to him. Normally, such a
thing took a little while. Gray Madison,
however, clearly had an appeal for
women of all ages; her included.

As they neared the vehicle at the
kerbside, she saw to her astonishment

that a child's seat was fitted in the rear. 'Oh.'

'I borrowed it from a friend who has children. He wasn't going to be using it for a day or two.' He shrugged, drawing her gaze, not for the first time, to the width of his shoulders. He had a powerful physique, an indication that he worked out on a regular basis. He lifted Daisy into the seat and strapped her in, before turning to Tara to assist her up into the passenger seat. Within a matter of moments, they were off.

'I like this car,' Daisy announced after a few moments. 'I can see everything.'

Which was a stark contrast to the low-slung Ferrari, from which you couldn't see much at all above pavement level.

'What animals will be at the farm?' Daisy went on.

'Well, now — let me see.' Gray pretended to give the matter some thought. 'I think they have some lambs and piglets. There are some goats who might have some kids. Hens, ducks . . . I believe there's a donkey, and a couple of Shetland ponies. There may even be a foal.'

'What's a foal?'

Gray met the child's gaze via his interior mirror. 'A young horse.'

Daisy clapped her hands in delight. It would be her idea of heaven, Tara decided. She swivelled her head and grinned at her niece.

Gray slanted a glance at Tara. 'I thought we'd have lunch first. There's a very good restaurant not far from the farm. It's in Stow-in-the-Wold. Would that suit you?'

'Oh, yes. Whatever you think. It's been years since I've been to the Cotswolds. My parents used to bring Ricky and me here.' Her voice faltered as emotion momentarily overwhelmed her. They'd had such happy times all together.

Gray reached out a hand and covered one of hers. 'I'm sorry. Are you sure you want to do this? We could go somewhere else.'

'Oh no. I'm looking forward to it, and we can't disappoint Daisy,' she softly added.

It didn't feel very long at all — although it was over an hour since they'd left the house — before they were parking in the central square of Stow and making their way towards the restaurant that Gray had mentioned. It was a historic black and white timbered building with pretty gardens surrounding it. They were packed with daffodils, narcissi, and drifts of late snowdrops and grape hyacinths. A few trees were also in blossom, their perfume drifting on the breeze towards Tara. She inhaled. 'Mmm, lovely.'

Gray turned his head to look at her. Daisy was hanging on to his hand. Tara grinned. 'You've obviously gained an admirer there.'

He didn't smile back. Instead, he murmured, 'And does her aunt feel the same way?' His smouldering gaze seared into her, setting her entire body ablaze.

Tara, lost for words, simply stared back at him.

'Clearly not,' he muttered.

Knowing she should say something, she stammered, 'We-ell, um, I barely know you.'

'We'll have to remedy that then, won't we?' And he smiled then. True, it wasn't a smile that reached his eyes, but it was a smile.

They walked into a large grey slate-floored hallway with several doors opening off it, one of which must be the restaurant. Gray took the first on the right of them, and sure enough there stood a beaming maître d'.

. 'I've reserved a table,' Gray told him. 'Madison is the name.'

'Certainly, Mr and Mrs Madison. And this must be your delightful daughter?' He smiled warmly down at Daisy.

'Oh no,' Tara hastened to correct him. 'I'm not — um, we're not — '

'We're not married,' Gray informed him.

Which, to Tara, made an already embarrassing situation even worse. Now the maître d' would think they were simply cohabiting. Although why that should embarrass her, she couldn't think. It was a pretty common occurrence these days.

'We're just friends,' she hurriedly put in, 'out for the day.'

The maître d' inclined his head. 'My mistake. I apologise. Now, would you like to come this way, please?' He led them to a table set for three.

'My daddy has gone away,' Daisy told Gray once they were seated, her blue eyes swimming with tears all of a sudden.

'Oh, I'm sorry, but I'm sure he'll be back soon.' Gray's gaze shifted to Tara, his expression a questioning one.

'We've left a note for him,' Daisy went on, 'in case he comes back while we're out.'

'That was a good idea. He'd probably worry if you weren't there.'

Daisy didn't answer. Instead, she

clutched at Gray's hand, which was resting on the table top. 'Do you have children?'

'I do. A son, Daniel. He's a bit older than you.'

'How old is he?'

'Nine.'

'Doesn't he live with you?'

'No, he lives mainly with his mother.'

Daisy frowned but didn't ask any more.

Once they had their drinks, a shandy for Gray, a white wine for Tara and a lemonade for Daisy, they began to study the menus. There was a children's menu, Tara was pleased to see.

'Daisy, would you like sausage and mashed potato?'

'Yes, please — with baked beans.'

With the preliminaries over and their meals ordered, Tara became aware of Gray's scrutiny. Feeling more confident after a couple of mouthfuls of her wine, she turned her head and returned his gaze.

'When do you hope to see your son

again?' She decided to keep the conversation a general one, hoping to ease the tension that had arisen between them.

'The Easter holidays — the end of April.'

'You must be looking forward to that.'

'I am. I'm not so sure that Daniel is, though.' Gray looked rueful. 'I suspect he'd much rather be with his friends.'

'Surely not.'

'You clearly don't know many nine-year-old boys.'

'Well, that's true. It's been a long time since Ricky was that age.'

'You said he was away — or rather Daisy did. On business?'

'No. Well, at least I don't think so. I suppose it could be that.' She frowned into her glass as she took another mouthful.

He cocked his head at her, his gaze a speculative one. 'Don't you know? Haven't you heard from him?'

'No.' She kept her voice low, not

wanting to worry Daisy. 'And it's been a fortnight now. Although it's been a habit of his to disappear for a while.'

His eyebrow lifted. It seemed a particular trait of his. 'I see.'

Their food was set before them at that point, to Tara's relief. She really didn't want to have to share her concerns over Ricky's welfare in front of Daisy. The little girl was already anxious enough about her father's whereabouts.

The meal was delicious, and they all cleared their plates; even Daisy, who could be picky on occasion. After ice creams all around, they left the restaurant and returned to the car, Daisy eagerly telling them what she wanted to do once they reached the farm.

'Well, I can hear that you've got it all well planned,' Gray remarked with a smile.

'Oh yes,' she gleefully told him. 'The lambs first, then the piglets, then — well, we'll see. I can't wait.' She clapped her hands together.

And she didn't have to wait long. Within fifteen minutes, they were driving through a gateway and along a winding driveway towards the gorgeous three-storey red-brick Georgian farmhouse that awaited them at the end.

'What a beautiful place,' Tara said.

'Yes, they're very proud of it. They've done an astonishing amount of work on it; it was pretty dilapidated.'

As they pulled to a halt on the circular forecourt, the front door opened and an attractive woman came out to greet them, blue eyes dancing with pleasure and a warm smile wreathing her face; she held her arms held out in welcome. A couple of dogs accompanied her; golden retrievers, Tara thought. She wasn't that well up on dog breeds.

'You must be Tara and Daisy,' she said. 'I'm Sophie, and these two here — ' She indicated the dogs, whose tails were wagging madly back and forth, every bit as pleased to see the three of them as their owner was. ' — are Tigger and

Maddie. They're child friendly.' She glanced reassuringly at Tara. 'So you don't need to worry.'

'Hello, how very nice to meet you.' Tara bent to stroke the two dogs who were as eager to greet the visitors as their owner was. She straightened up to look at her niece, who was standing back a little, visibly unsure about these two large animals bouncing about her. 'Say hello, Daisy.' But Daisy still looked nervous as she stood once more clutching Gray's hand.

'They won't hurt you, Daisy,' he assured her. 'Look, pat their heads — like this. They love little girls.'

And astonishingly, Daisy did, chortling in delight when the two animals licked her chubby fingers.

'Okay,' Sophie began, 'now what do you want to do first? Go and see the animals, or come inside the house and have a drink? Gray?' She turned easily to him, obviously knowing him well. A fact she confirmed by telling Tara, 'We're old friends, aren't we, Gray?

Gray and John, my husband, were at school together in Oxford. It was an amazing coincidence that we all ended up in this area.' She smiled down at Daisy. 'So what's it going to be?'

'To see the animals, please,' Daisy whispered, still clinging to Gray.

Tara, however, could see the excitement simmering within the little girl, despite her display of shyness. She laughed and became instantly aware of Gray's gaze moving to her, warming with admiration as it did so.

'Okay,' he softly said. 'The animals it is, then.'

10

Daisy was instantly smitten with the animals. She was handed a bottle of milk to give to a lamb, which she did with a truly astonishing skill for a mere five-year-old, after which they moved from animal to animal, Daisy all the while looking as if she'd been granted admission to heaven.

Eventually, she was persuaded to say goodbye to them all and return to the farmhouse, where Sophie provided coffee for the three adults and home-made apple juice for Daisy, along with a plateful of delicious homemade scones and cream. They sat in a huge kitchen around an equally huge table, and chatted until it was time to say their goodbyes. John arrived just as they were leaving and insisted that the four of them meet up one evening in the not too distant future for a meal together.

Tara was overwhelmed by it all. Sophie and John were clearly assuming that Gray and Tara were an established couple, although nothing had been said to that effect. Which made her wonder what Gray had told them about her. She stared at him in the wake of John's invitation, unsure what to say, and was almost completely undone when Gray returned her stare and grinned, his eyes dancing as he asked her, 'Is that okay with you, Tara?'

All she could do was nod her consent, words temporarily beyond her, despite the fact that she was feeling decidedly cornered into agreeing.

Gray turned to John and said, 'Okay. I'll ring you and we'll set something up.'

* * *

The journey back to Mallow End didn't seem to take long at all, mainly because Daisy, in her usual lively fashion, chattered non-stop all the way. Gray exhibited a great deal of patience, answering her litany of questions easily and confidently until Daisy asked, completely out of the blue, 'Do you like Auntie Tara?'

He paused, as if giving serious consideration to the question — which would have thrown the majority of men, Tara decided — before saying, with a slanted glance at a rosy-cheeked Tara, 'Yes, I do — very much.'

Daisy then turned a guileless smile upon Tara. 'Do you like Gray, Auntie Tara?'

Tara felt her face warm at that point. Nonetheless, she managed to disregard Gray's grin of uninhibited anticipation to say, 'Of course. Why wouldn't I?'

She also then managed to ignore his softly murmured, 'Indeed, why wouldn't you?'

She did turn her head then to glare at him, which only provoked a deep-throated chuckle and the by-now familiar raising of one eyebrow.

'That's good.' Daisy gave a sigh of contentment. ''Cause I like him, too.'

Gray's gaze moved to the interior mirror as he regarded the supremely satisfied child in the back. 'Well,' he murmured, 'with that all cleared up, might I suggest that we carry this on into the evening?' He glanced sideways at Tara. 'Would — um, Lizzie, isn't it; your friend's name?' Tara nodded. 'Babysit while I take you out for supper?'

'Oh.' That was the last thing she'd expected.

He again raised an eyebrow at her look of confusion. 'Problem?'

'Well, could be. Lizzie likes to keep Sunday for the family.'

'Ah, I see.'

Tara turned to him. He appeared genuinely disappointed. 'Look — why don't you stay and I'll cook us something?' He'd been so very generous taking them out as he had, it seemed the least she could do. And, if she was being totally honest with herself, she didn't want the day to end either.

'Oh goody, goody.' Daisy clapped her hands joyfully.

'Oh no, missy.' Tara swivelled her head to look at the beaming little girl. 'It's school tomorrow. So it's a light supper for you and then a bath and bed.'

'No.' Daisy pouted at her. 'That's not fair.'

Gray regarded her once again via the interior mirror. 'If you're a good girl, then I promise we'll have another day out just like this one.'

'Promise? Really?' Mollified by this, she beamed at him.

He smiled back. 'I promise.'

Her smile disappeared momentarily as she asked, 'You won't do what daddy does, will you? Break your promise?'

He considered her for a long moment before saying, 'I won't do that, Daisy. But maybe Daddy couldn't help it. Sometimes other things get in the way of what we really want to do.'

But this time Daisy wasn't to be appeased. She folded her arms firmly across her small chest, frowning at him as she muttered, 'He always does it. And now he's gone away.' Her lower lip quivered.

It was Tara's turn to say, 'He'll be back, darling. It must have been something very important to keep him away.'

Mercifully, at that point, Gray pulled up in front of the house. 'Here we are,' he said. 'Home again.'

* * *

The business of going inside, showing Gray into the sitting room, and putting together a sandwich successfully distracted Daisy's thoughts away from the failings of her father, and pretty soon she was once more chattering nineteen to the dozen to an attentive Gray.

It took a bit of doing, but eventually Tara persuaded her niece up the stairs and into her bedroom, where she then coaxed an increasingly fretful little girl into bed.

'I want Gray to come and say good night.'

'Oh, well . . . ' Tara was loath to ask him to do even more for them. He'd done more than enough that day, in her opinion.

'Ple-ease.'

Tara went out onto the landing and called down the stairs, 'Gray, would you mind? Daisy wants to say good night.'

With no sign of any sort of exasperation — unlike Ricky, who frequently demonstrated just that, or more often than not, point-blank refused — Gray came up and strode into the bedroom. Daisy was tucked up under her quilt, but she held out both arms to him. He went to her and bent down to plant a kiss upon her cheek. 'Good night, Daisy. It's been a real pleasure to meet you.'

Daisy, naturally, smiled with happiness. 'It's been a pleasure to meet you, too.'

He laughed and kissed her again. She took instant advantage of that and wound both arms up and around his neck, holding him down against her. 'You promise you'll take me out again?' she whispered.

'I promise.'

'You've been very patient,' Tara told him once they were back in the sitting room. 'It's just what she needed. Thank you.'

'Why wouldn't I have been patient? She's a lovely little girl. You must be proud of her.'

'I am. I just wish . . . ' Her words limped into silence.

'You wish?'

'I wish her father was the same.'

'What's the problem, Tara?' His tone was one of gentle compassion.

She shrugged. 'I wish I knew. Ricky's always been unreliable. It's not the first time he's just taken off without telling me where he's going. I thought at first it was because of our parents dying while he was still young, and I suppose I over-compensated for that, but . . . '

'But?'

'Well, he's a grown man now; he's twenty-three, and a father. He should have developed some sort of sense of responsibility, instead of — '

'Instead of leaving the role of parent to you?'

'Yes.' Was she saying too much again? But she couldn't keep making excuses for Ricky. And somehow, however belatedly she'd reached this conclusion, she didn't think Gray would pass judgement on her over her brother's behaviour; something which, after all, she had no control over. 'Don't misunderstand me, I love Daisy and I don't mind in the least looking after her, but I do want him to be more a father to her. She needs that, a man in her life.'

'He's relatively young. Give him time. I'm sure he will be.'

'I wish.' She sighed. 'Anyway, enough of that. Can I offer you a drink? It's wine or wine, I'm afraid. Although I might be lucky and find a beer in the fridge.'

'Wine's fine.'

'Red or white? I can at least offer that choice.'

'A glass of red would be great. And look, please don't feel you have to cook for me. Lunch was very substantial.'

She poured and then handed him a glass of Merlot. 'Cheese and biscuits?'

'Perfect. But let's just sit and drink our wine first. There's no rush, is there? Unless you want me to go?' His gaze narrowed at her.

'Oh no, good heavens. You've given us such a lovely day. I'm so grateful.' She was gushing, she could hear. *Stop it*, she told herself. *You're beginning to sound like a gauche teenager.*

'Are you?' His words were so low, she barely heard them.

'Yes.' She gulped her wine down. There was no mistaking the expression in his eye. He didn't have to actually ask the question. It was, 'How grateful?' She hurriedly changed the subject. She didn't want the evening to end with the same sort of unpleasantness she'd experienced with Mark. Not that she thought it would; not really. Gray didn't seem the type. Even so, she couldn't be a hundred percent sure about that.

'I like your friends very much. Do they not have children?' She was gabbling now, rather than gushing, so heightened were her emotions. Which were only intensified by the fact that Gray wasn't saying anything. He simply sat there, his gaze still narrowed and still riveted upon her. What did he intend? Something, that was very evident. To make love to her? Did she want that? The honest answer to that question was, she didn't know. Her best bet was to keep him talking; deflect him from whatever it was he had in mind.

'No. It's a great sadness to them both.'

'I'm sorry. They'd make wonderful parents, I'm sure.'

'I imagine they would.' His tone was a dry one now. Amusement glinted at her along with the gold flecks she'd spotted more than once. Quite what they signified, she hadn't a clue. But the truth was, he knew what she was doing, and most probably, exactly what she was thinking.

She leapt to her feet. 'I'll get the cheese and biscuits. I think I *am* hungry, after all.' And she fled to the kitchen.

Of course, he wasn't about to let her get away with that — she should have known he wouldn't — so he got to his feet and followed her. 'I'll give you a hand.'

His voice came from right behind her as she stood at the kitchen worktop. She jumped with surprise and swivelled, to find him standing a mere inch behind her. So close, in fact, their chests were touching. A stab of heat ran straight through her. 'Oh,' she gasped.

Gray didn't move back. Instead, his gaze bore into her, smouldering, hot. 'You must know how attracted I am to you,' he huskily said.

'A-are you?'

'Yes.' He lowered his head towards

hers. His lips were only an inch away. She felt his arm slide about her waist, drawing her closer; his breath feathered the skin of her face, inducing a shaft of hot desire right through her. 'And I'm hoping you feel the same way.' His voice was husky; seductive.

'I-I do-don't.'

He didn't allow her the time to finish because his mouth captured hers in a kiss that was full of hunger, passion, need and a desire fully the equal of hers.

Tara couldn't help herself. She parted her lips to him, letting his tongue inside to tangle with hers. Her body flamed, the very core of her seeming to dissolve into molten liquid.

He deepened the kiss as his hand slid over her back, caressing, touching, tracing the curve of her hip, cupping the fullness he found there. It wasn't until his fingers moved upwards once more, finding her breast, his thumb gently flicking the peak, that sanity returned and she realised what it was she was permitting him to do.

She was no better than all the other women he'd probably made love to in the same fashion. He was certainly demonstrating a highly practised skill in the art of lovemaking. Determined not to be just one more of many, she tugged away, at the same time pushing his hands from her. 'Please — don't.'

He instantly took a step back, his hands dropping to his sides as he lifted his head to look at her. He was frowning, puzzled. 'Why not?'

'It's not right.'

'Why not?' He repeated the question, his frown deepening. He was watching her closely. 'I'm a man, you're a woman. An ideal combination, in my opinion.'

'No. I haven't got time for a relationship.' She only just stopped herself from adding, 'and certainly not with my boss.' She'd always had a strict policy of not becoming involved with an employer or a fellow employee. If it went wrong, as it invariably did — or so she'd heard from others who'd gone down that particular route — she'd almost certainly be out of a job. As she was already on sticky ground as far as that was concerned, she didn't want to worsen the situation.

'Are you sure about that?'

'Yes, really — I haven't. All my free time is taken up with Daisy, and-and she has to come first. I'm sorry.'

His features darkened. 'So, tell me exactly — where does her father feature in this? In fact, come to think of it, does he feature at all? Because, so far, there's absolutely no evidence that he actually exists.'

His tone was a scornful one, and it sliced right through Tara. My God. He believed she was lying. Which seemed to indicate that he was also beginning to believe that Daisy could be hers.

11

'Well, I can assure you he does. You've heard as much from Daisy. Or do you believe she's fabricated him as well?' He had the grace to look a little sheepish at that. Especially when she went on, 'As I've said, I don't know where he is.' Tara stumbled to a halt. 'He-he's totally vanished.'

'Vanished?' His expression then was one of concern rather than scorn.

'Yes. At least, I haven't been able to track him down.' Her indignation at his initial scepticism, if not disbelief of what she was telling him, melted away. 'He's not answering his phone — well, I think he's turned it off. So he's not receiving my calls.' Her voice broke then. 'I-I don't know what to think; what to do.'

Gray regarded her in silence for a moment or two, his features and his tone softening as he asked, 'How long did you say he's been gone?'

'A fortnight.'

'Have you informed the police?'

'I did, a couple of days after he didn't come home, but they weren't interested. He's a grown man, they said.' She shrugged her shoulders, 'which he is, but . . .'

'Well, I think you should ring them again.'

She frowned and nibbled at her lower lip. 'I don't really want to do that.'

'Why not?' His gaze narrowed with suspicion now, rather than disbelief.

'I'm afraid he might be in some sort of trouble.'

Gray continued to stare at her. 'Why would you think that?'

'I don't know, but . . .' Again her words limped into silence.

'But?'

'I get the impression that he's been mixing with a few dodgy characters, one of whom seems to be searching for him.' She bit at her bottom lip. She was telling him too much judging, by the expression on his face.

'And you know that how?'

'A man has phoned here a couple of times, asking for Ricky.' She didn't intend to tell him about the threat. If she did that, he'd most likely take matters into his own hands and ring the police. And, as she'd decided several times now, she couldn't risk that happening and the police beginning an investigation, for fear of what they might uncover. 'Anyway, all that aside, as I said, I really can't embark on any sort of relationship.'

'Okay. In that case, when that situation changes, maybe you'll let me know.' His tone as well as his expression warmed as he regarded her. 'The truth is, I'm really attracted to you, Tara. I believe we could have something good; something lasting. But for now,' he hastily added upon spotting her nervousness at the turn his words had taken, 'we'll take things one step at a time — if that's what you really want?'

Tara nodded.

'So when can I see you again, on a purely friendly basis, naturally?' he added for good measure. 'With Sophie and John if it makes you feel more comfortable?'

'Oh?' He'd genuinely surprised her. She'd expected him to walk away from her. 'I-I thought — '

'What?'

'Well, that you wouldn't want to see me again?'

'That would be a bit difficult, seeing as you work for me. In any case,' he added as he watched her from beneath lowered lids, 'I think you're worth spending time on; waiting for, in other words. Shall I ring you when I've arranged something definite with Sophie and John?'

Again, she nodded her consent.

'Right, so I'll forego the cheese, if you don't mind, and leave.'

'Oh.' Was that all she could say? Oh? Surely she could come up with something a little more imaginative. But the truth was, his sudden decision to leave was a surprising one, and her expression must have revealed something of that. Because he went on, in little more than a low mutter, 'The truth is, I don't think I've got the strength of will to sit a couple of feet away from you and merely *look*.'

Tara was forced to hide a smile at that. She wasn't sure she'd been meant to hear those final words. What they meant, of course, was that he wouldn't be able to resist making love to her.

A thrill shot right through her at the mere thought of that, and she was sorely tempted, there and then, to ask him to stay. She couldn't deny that she was deeply attracted to him, too. But until she knew where Ricky was, she couldn't concentrate upon any sort of love affair. And even then, she'd have to make a decision. Would it be altogether wise to change her long-held policy and embark upon a relationship with the man who was her employer? At the moment, she had no idea what her answer to that would be.

She led him to the door and stood, watching him leave. So she saw the exact moment that the Range Rover pulled away from the house and another car approached from the opposite direction. It stopped as Gray passed and dipped its headlights before performing a speedy U-turn and driving off in the same direction as Gray was going.

Tara lifted both hands to her lips. That looked like the identical car to the one that had been parked across the road from her house. Could whoever was driving it be following Gray, thinking it might be Ricky? But surely he would know that Ricky couldn't possibly afford a car like that? Unless her suspicions were correct and Ricky was involved in some sort of criminal activity? In which case, he could probably well afford such a luxurious car.

But that aside, she needed to know that Gray was safe. She waited fifteen minutes for him to reach Osborne

House, and then she tried his mobile number. He answered immediately. She breathed a soft sigh of relief.

'Tara? Is something wrong?'

'No. I-I just wanted to know you'd got home safely.'

There was a short silence, then, 'Well, I'm fine. I only had one glass of wine.' She could hear that he was smiling. 'But it's immensely encouraging to know you care.'

'Right.'

'So is that it?'

'Yes.'

'Okay. Good night, then. I'll be in touch. Um . . . ' He paused. 'If you're at all troubled or worried about anything, anything at all, ring me, okay? Any time, day or night.'

'I will. Thank you.'

★   ★   ★

It was the rattling of the letterbox and a short, sharp ringing of the doorbell that awoke Tara in the early hours of the following morning. She squinted at the clock on her bedside table. Six o'clock? Who on earth could that be? It was far too early for the postman.

She sat up, listening intently for any further sounds. Could it be Ricky? But he wouldn't ring the bell; he had a door key. Which meant it must be someone else. Her mystery phone caller? But why would he be here, at her door, at this time of the morning, ringing the bell?

She climbed out of bed as quietly as she could and shrugged on her dressing gown. Then, still without making a sound, she crept down the stairs, all the while listening for any other sounds. A door opening; a window breaking. Reassuringly, she heard nothing at all.

It wasn't until she reached the hallway that she saw the envelope lying on the doormat. There was no name or address on it, so it had to have been hand delivered. That had been the reason for the ringing of the bell, supposedly. A shiver of misgiving went through her as she hurried across to it and picked it up, and then, with fingers that quivered, opened it and pulled out the single sheet of paper inside. She unfolded it and gave a low, despairing moan as she read what was written upon it.

WE WANT OUR GOODS BACK OR THE MONEY FOR THEM. HE'S GOT 48 HOURS OR WE TAKE SOMETHING OF HIS. TELL HIM.

The written words, rather than the sound of someone's voice speaking them, made them all the more menacing. Had that been his intention? If so, it had worked. Despite the early hour, she tried ringing her brother's number. In vain, as always. His phone must still be turned off, as it had been for over two weeks. How could he do this? Didn't he care about her and Daisy? Especially Daisy? He must know they would both worry about him. Just as he must be aware of what was happening to them if he'd gone to the lengths of disappearing to escape the man — or men — searching for him. She couldn't be sure it was always the same man watching the house, although the car looked the same.

What had he taken with him? Something of great value. It had to be, for someone to be so determined to get it back that they'd be making such threats. There was one consolation to be had from all of this. She didn't think whoever it was — one man or more — would harm him, not before they'd retrieved whatever it was he'd taken. She didn't dare consider what they might be driven to do if they failed in that goal.

For the umpteenth time, she asked herself if she should disregard her fears and ring the police. But what if they hunted Ricky down and arrested him? Which seemed the most likely outcome.

She'd wait a little longer. Because, after all, what could her mystery caller do if Ricky didn't contact him? Or her? They couldn't hurt him if they couldn't find him.

But it didn't take long for Tara to realise exactly what the anonymous caller could do.

Gray rang her on Tuesday afternoon at the salon. It was just after lunch. 'I've spoken to John and arranged for the four of us to meet on Saturday evening, seven thirty, at The Brasserie just outside of Abbotsleigh. Is that okay for you? I can change it.'

Tara didn't know it, having never been there, but she had no hesitation in saying, 'No — that's fine. But isn't it a bit far for Sophie and John to come for a meal and then drive home again?'

'They'll spend the night at mine.'

'Oh, right.'

'Are you okay, Tara? You don't sound yourself.'

'I'm still worried about my brother. He hasn't come back or even phoned me. It's been over two weeks now.' She made no mention of the threatening letter she'd received. She knew what his

response would be. Ring the police
— now.

'Do you want me to come to the salon? Is there anything I can do?'

'No, there's no need for that. I'm sure he's okay. I'm probably worrying needlessly. I expect he'll simply walk through the door and wonder why I've been concerned, knowing Ricky.' She tried a laugh but, embarrassingly, it erupted as a squeak.

'I'm coming over.'

'No, really, I'm fine. I'll see you on Saturday.'

She returned to her client, who was having a nail treatment.

'Everything okay?' the woman asked. 'You don't look too well.'

'I'm fine. A spot of family bother, that's all. I'm sure it'll sort itself out.' *If only*, she thought. 'Now have you decided on the colour varnish you want?'

She was carefully applying the base coat before adding the shade of bronze that the client had selected when she felt the back of her neck begin to tingle. She stopped what she was doing and put a hand up to it, smoothing the skin and turning her head from side to side, in an attempt to ease the tightness that she guessed was the direct result of the amount of stress and tension she was experiencing. She'd also done four other treatments this morning, two full massages and two complete nail treatments, on both fingers and toes. Her neck and back were both stiff, as were her shoulders. She straightened up momentarily and stretched her back, wriggling her shoulders at the same time.

It was then that Annie called across to her from where she standing at the reception desk, having just taken a phone call. 'Tara, there's a man outside. He's staring in here — looks a bit of a bruiser. Do you know him?'

Tara instantly swivelled to look out of the window, and, sure enough, saw a thickset man, not particularly tall, maybe five feet nine or ten, dressed in some sort of jacket; leather, she thought. He had pockmarked cheeks and an elaborate tattoo running up the side of his neck, and he was standing just outside of the salon, looking in through the window, staring straight at her. Even as she excused herself to her client and began to walk towards the door, he swung and strode quickly away.

She broke into a run then and opened the door, hurrying outside, slightly fearfully it had to be said, because it was a bit of a coincidence that on the day after she'd received the threat giving Ricky forty-eight hours to return whatever it was he'd taken, a sinister-looking man should show up here. She strode outside and looked down the road in the direction that he'd gone. Sadly — or maybe not, because what would she have said or done if he'd still been hanging around? — he'd vanished as suddenly as he'd arrived. But it had to have been the same man who'd been phoning her, didn't it? He hadn't looked like a prospective client. Far from it. She couldn't imagine he'd ever received a massage in the whole of his life. It didn't look as if he visited a hairdresser very often, either. His hair, a dirty shade of blond, had overlapped the collar of his jacket and flopped untidily down over his brow, partially concealing his face.

She walked slowly inside again, deep in thought. If it had been him, had he had another message for Ricky, but upon seeing her, along with several others, changed his mind? Yet why come to the salon in the first place and allow himself to be seen? To intensify the pressure on her to contact Ricky? He clearly believed she knew where he was. She sighed. If only she did.

Annie again called across to her, 'Who was it? Do you know him?'

Tara shook her head. 'No. How long had he been standing there?'

'A couple of minutes, no longer. The second you headed for him he was off, like a rat out of a trap. Strange, huh?'

'Yeah. It was probably nothing. Just someone having a nose.'

But as she returned to her by now curious client, a growing sense of unease, of undeniable menace, filled her. What had he wanted? To see her? But if so, why hadn't he come in? No. His intention had been, in the wake of the written threat, to deepen her fear, to literally terrify her into contacting Ricky. What other reason could he have had?

Tara passed the rest of the day in a state of concealed, she hoped, agitation. The forty-eight hours that Ricky had been given to return whatever it was he had taken would be up in the early hours of the next morning.

So it wasn't surprising that by the time six o'clock arrived and she could close the salon for the day, she felt on the verge of a complete breakdown.

'Tara, are you all right?' Annie asked. 'You've looked worried all day. Is there something wrong? With Daisy?'

'I-I'm fine. Just tired. I haven't been

sleeping well. Look — I must go. I'll see you tomorrow. Will you lock up?' And she dashed from the salon, leaving Annie still frowning behind her.

She collected Daisy from Lizzie's.

'You're looking a bit frazzled, love,' Lizzie remarked with a searching glance. 'Bad day? Stay and have a glass of wine.'

'No, I can't,' Tara told her. 'I need to get home.'

The second she walked through the front door, she tried Ricky's number again, with the same result as always. No response. She followed this with yet another text message, just in case her brother still had possession of his phone and should bother checking it at some point. 'Ring me' was all it said.

Daisy, not surprisingly, had started to pick up on her aunt's agitated state of mind, refusing to eat her poached egg and even turning down the offer of a choc ice. Tara didn't know what to do for the best. Simply wait for what was about to happen, contact the police, and risk a criminal investigation? Or ring her closest friend, Bel? She had her mobile phone in her hand to do just that when the front doorbell chimed.

Her heart lurched.

Oh, please God, let it be Ricky. Although why he'd be ringing the bell, she didn't know. It couldn't be him, she told herself as she ran to the front window. Could it be her mystery caller? Rather than phoning, had he decided to pay her a visit? Confront her? But the forty-eight hours weren't up yet. Her heartbeat increased significantly, quickening both her breathing and her pulse rate, as she peered out and saw the red Ferrari parked at the kerbside.

Gray. It was Gray.

In a way, that was a relief. She'd dreaded seeing the same man as earlier. But what would she tell Gray? He was here, she was sure, with more questions about Ricky. She couldn't tell him the truth: the letter, the threat — the sheer menace and intimidation of the strange man's visit to the salon. He'd insist she ring the police and she couldn't, she simply couldn't.

She walked into the hallway and opened the door.

'Is he back?' His piercing gaze seemed to penetrate right through her. 'Obviously not.'

Tara gave a grim smile. No beating about the bush then? No polite preliminaries? What chance did she have of keeping anything from this man?

'No.' She turned back into the house. Gray followed her into the sitting room. Daisy, who'd been watching the television, leapt to her feet the second she spied Gray. 'Gray, Gray,' she cried.

'Hello there.' Gray smiled down at her. 'How are you?'

'I'm fine.' She frowned. 'But I don't think Auntie Tara is.' And she swept her anxious gaze to Tara.

'Well, I'm here to try and make that better.' Gray, too, regarded her.

'Drink?' Desperate by this time, Tara sought refuge from the piercing gaze that felt as if it were burning into her, practically searing her flesh as it did so. Fetching the glasses, she hoped that a bottle of wine would prove an effective — if temporary — distraction from the fact that this man was once again standing in her house looking for all the world as if he belonged there.

'That sounds good. A glass of wine is just what we need.' And still his gaze was glued upon her, the gleam in his eye an indication that he knew only too well what she was doing, but that he was willing to go along with her.

'Red?'

'Perfect.'

She headed for the kitchen as Daisy said, with yet another demonstration of her quaintly old-world charm, 'Please, sit down, Gray.'

'Thank you, I will.' Tara smiled to herself, her smile widening as she heard Gray reply, 'Tell me about your day at school.'

'Talking about school, young lady,' Tara said upon re-entering the room, holding two glasses with one hand and the bottle of wine with the other, 'it's time for bed.'

'Ooh, not yet. Gray's only just come.'

'Five minutes then, no more. It's gone seven o'clock.'

Daisy pouted, but once her five minutes were up, she stood and said, 'Will you come and tuck me in, Gray?'

'I certainly will. It's not often I get to tuck a gorgeous young lady into her bed.' And he slanted a glittering, overtly sensuous gaze at Tara. 'Give me a shout when you're ready.'

And that was exactly what happened. Daisy was well-practised in the arts of undressing herself and brushing her teeth, and so was done in five minutes.

'Gray,' she called.

'I'm coming,' Gray called back.

'Thank you,' Tara said as he exited the room.

'No problem.'

But there clearly was because, he was gone for almost ten minutes. Tara was about to go upstairs to see what was going on when he arrived back in the sitting room.

'We had to have a story, but she's clearly tired.'

'Yes. School does her in. Lord knows what she gets up to there.'

Tara was sitting on the settee where she usually sat, in the corner from where she could view the television. It wasn't until Gray picked up his glass from the table where he'd left it and came to sit alongside her that Tara conceded she might have made a mistake. There was a smouldering warmth about him that he was making no attempt to conceal.

She inched away from him, nestling further into her corner. But when he made no move to get closer, she felt herself relaxing. She firmly disregarded the small curl of disappointment, and instead prepared herself for the questions to begin.

It didn't take long. He took a generous mouthful of his wine and asked, 'No word from your brother then?'

'No.' She also indulged in a large

gulp of her wine; her excuse — she needed it to steady her nerves.

'And you're still not prepared to call the police?'

'No. I can't rid myself of the suspicion that he's got himself into a bit of bother.'

'Criminal bother, I'm assuming you mean?'

She nodded.

'You really think he'd be capable of something like that?'

She shrugged.

'I'll take that as a maybe, shall I?' He continued to regard her from beneath lowered eyelids. 'Has he done anything like this before?'

'What? Disappearing? Yes, but not for this length of time.'

'Actually, I didn't mean the disappearing act. You've already mentioned that it's not the first time. I was referring to your suspicion of some sort of criminal activity.'

'I don't think so, but . . . ' Again, she shrugged. 'I don't really know. He wouldn't have told me if he had.'

'So why would you think he's capable of that now?'

'Because of the phone calls. He's taken something that belongs to the caller and he wants it back.'

'What?'

'I don't know.'

He cocked his head as he continued to consider her. 'I understand your quandary, but wouldn't it be better to find out? What if something's happened to him? He could be injured; have you considered that possibility?'

'I've tried to put it out of my mind, if you want the truth.'

'Tara, it's always better to know the truth. You can begin to deal with it then.'

'Not if it's a serious crime. If he's stolen something of value, something which clearly this man badly wants back . . . ' She gnawed at her lip. She hadn't intended telling him quite so much. 'I've had an anonymous letter as well.' She paused. In for a penny, in for a pound. 'Also, I'm pretty sure someone's been watching the house.'

'And you've still not informed the police?' His tone was an angry one now. His expression had darkened; his eyes were mere slits. 'You — or Daisy — could be in real danger. If this person is some sort of criminal.'

She hadn't thought of that aspect of things. Oh God. Had she laid herself and Daisy open to harm?

'H-he said in the letter that Ricky had forty-eight hours to return.'

'Or what?'

'He didn't say.' But of course he had. He'd told her he'd take something of Ricky's. Something precious to him. A fair exchange, as he'd put it. Her heart lurched, as did her stomach; and once again, she wondered if he could possibly mean her.

'When will the forty-eight hours be up?'

'Tomorrow morning, early.'

He pulled out his phone from his shirt pocket.

'Wh-what are you doing?'

'Phoning the police. This can't go on.'

'No, please,' she begged. 'Let me wait until tomorrow. Ricky might still return. I've texted him, and I can't bear to think the police will start a manhunt. Daisy will be heartbroken, and she's upset enough as it is.' Tears filled her eyes as her mouth quivered. 'Please.'

'But what if one of you is hurt?'

'We won't be.' She crossed her fingers behind her back, praying she was right. She was positive it wasn't Daisy he was threatening to take; if it was anyone, it would be her. But surely he wouldn't do that? It would almost certainly start a police investigation, and that must be the last thing he'd want. 'It's Ricky and whatever he's taken with him that he wants.'

'Well, okay, but if he's not back by the morning, if you don't ring the police, I will.'

She lifted her glass to her lips and drained it. Her hand shook as she replaced it on the coffee table.

'Come here,' Gray said. He put his glass down, a glass that unlike Tara's was still half full. He slid across the settee towards her and put an arm around her shoulders. Tara couldn't stop herself. She nestled against him. It was so good to have someone holding her; comforting her.

He put his other arm around her then, encircling her completely, holding her tenderly and close.

'It's okay. We'll sort something out.' His voice shook too.

Surprised, Tara lifted her head and looked at him. He gave a helpless groan as he bent his head towards hers. 'I'm sorry,' he muttered hoarsely, 'but I can't help myself.' And before she had any chance of pulling away, his mouth had covered hers, and his kiss, gentle to start with, deepened into one that took her breath away.

12

Equally as helpless as Gray beneath the tidal wave of desire, Tara found herself passionately responding. Her hand slid upwards over his chest to rest upon the nape of his neck, where she twisted her fingers in amongst the silky strands of his hair, loving the sensual feel of it against her fingertips.

His probing tongue parted her lips, moving within to tangle with hers, as he pressed her backwards into the cushions until she was practically lying beneath him. His mouth left hers then and gently rested on her closed eyelids before tracing a path down her cheek and arched throat to locate the wildly throbbing pulse at the base.

It was her turn now to softly groan as every nerve ending in her body went wild and a fiery heat flamed within her stomach, threatening to consume her as she relinquished herself to his lovemaking.

His fingers found the buttons of her blouse and began to unfasten them, and suddenly she was struggling free of it and then her bra. Her skirt had already ridden up, exposing her shapely thighs.

'Oh God,' Gray moaned, 'you're beautiful — I want you so much.'

Tara felt his fingers caressing her, tenderly but passionately, as they stroked and cupped. Once again, she was helpless against her own desire. Nothing else mattered. Nothing. All the disturbing events that had been happening to her — the phone calls, the letter, the stalking — were forgotten; her brother's disappearance, her own fear . . . all forgotten, for the moment, at least. So when Gray muttered, 'Can we move somewhere more comfortable?' she made no demur. There was no point denying her own needs, her intense desire for him, either to him or herself. She wanted him every bit as much as he wanted her. She couldn't fight it any longer. She wriggled from beneath him and, holding out her hand, murmured, 'Come with me.'

She led him quickly and quietly up the stairs to her bedroom, telling herself they were both adults, capable of making and acting upon their own decisions. And whatever the consequences should turn out to be, she'd — they'd — deal with them.

She pulled off her remaining garments and watched as Gray did the same, exposing the perfection of his body; powerful, gorgeous — *Wow!* she silently exclaimed. How would any woman be able to resist that?

'Are you sure about this?' he asked.

'Yes.' She put from her mind her former fears of any sort of romantic involvement with an employer. She needed this every bit as much as he did. It had been a long time since she'd made love with a man; far too long.

She lay on the bed and held her arms out to him. He wasted no time in joining her.

Their lovemaking was glorious, fulfilling every one of Tara's expectations. It was tender yet passionate, demanding at times, yet gentle, and it went on and on. Eventually, in the early hours, sated and completely satisfied, they fell asleep, wrapped lovingly around each other, arms and legs entwined, to be eventually woken by the sounds of Daisy moving around in her own room.

'What time is it?' Tara gasped.

Gray was propped up on his pillows, smiling down at her, and clearly wide awake. 'Seven o'clock.'

'How long have you been awake?'

'Half an hour or so. You looked so peaceful, I didn't have the heart to wake you.'

Tara's face flamed. Had he been looking at her for half an hour? She glanced down over herself. The duvet was sitting low against her stomach. Her entire torso was exposed.

He gave a throaty chuckle. 'No need to look so anxious. You have nothing to be ashamed of.' He bent over her and dropped a kiss, first on one breast, then the other. 'You're totally gorgeous; irresistible, in fact. And . . . ' Now he looked embarrassed, a faint flush tingeing his face.

'And?' she playfully teased him.

He stared at her. 'And — I'm in love with you.'

The words, as simply said as they were, for a second time took her breath clean away.

'And have been since the first moment I saw you standing in front of me, clutching your jars, your bottles, your towels.' He smiled shakily at her. 'You were adorable. And those eyes — so huge, so glorious, staring at me. Don't you realise the effect you have? You completely conquered me.'

Tara too now sat up, staring at him and then watching as his breathing halted and his eyes softened, as he watched her drawing the quilt up around herself. She couldn't speak for a long, long moment, hardly daring to believe what it was he was telling her.

He loved her. He actually loved her. She too now took a deep breath. She'd been afraid to say the words the night before in case he hadn't felt the same way. But now, 'I love you too,' she softly told him.

'Oh, Tara.' He wrapped his arms around her to hold her close, so close she could feel every beat of his heart. 'Let me look after you and Daisy. You seem so alone.'

She sighed, nestling against him. 'I feel it at the moment.'

'Well, not anymore, never anymore.' He bent his head to kiss her at the exact second that Daisy called, 'Auntie Tara, can I come in? I'm dressed.'

'Oh.' Tara glanced diffidently at Gray.

'I'm okay with that — if you are? We're both decent.'

And they were, both of them now with the duvet up to their shoulders.

'She has to know,' Gray murmured.

Tara still hesitated. Daisy had never seen her with a man before, and certainly not in bed with one. But Daisy took matters into her own hands and opened the door and walked into the room. She stopped dead as she spotted Gray alongside Tara.

'Did you stay all night?' She stood, legs apart, hands on her hips, frowning darkly at them both. Tara felt for all the world like a wicked child caught out in some terrible misdeed.

Gray, however, took the whole thing in his stride, his expression untroubled and smiling. 'I did. Your aunt was lonely.'

'Oh, that's okay then,' Daisy blithely assured him, performing an instant about-turn from highly critical to smiling satisfaction. 'She needs a husband.'

Tara didn't know whether to be amused or horrified. 'Daisy — ?'

'Well, you do. Lizzie's always telling you to get a move on and find yourself a good man.'

And with that, Tara lost any remaining remnants of self-control and broke into laughter. 'Well.' She slanted a glance at Gray, who was lying back against the pillows also helpless with laughter. 'That's telling me.'

'So, come on — get up,' Daisy briskly went on, 'or I'll be late for school.'

★   ★   ★

Tara went to work, determined to put her fears for Ricky to one side. She had Gray now; she wasn't alone anymore. Somehow, between them, she was sure they'd deal with whatever the next few hours threw at them.

Annie gave her a long, considering look. 'Someone looks better. What's happened? Don't tell me — you've won the lottery?'

'I wish. Mind you as I never play it, that's highly unlikely. No, I just had a good night's sleep.' Which, of course, was a complete fabrication. She'd barely slept at all. She and Gray hadn't been able to get enough of each other. However, she wasn't about to share that snippet of information with anyone.

In any case, when she looked at the appointment book and saw that they were solidly booked all day, she decided she had no time for chatting. Not that she was complaining. The salon's future was beginning to look way more secure. A lot of their formerly regular clients were steadily returning to them. She smiled to herself. Not that she thought Gray would get rid of her now, not with all that was happening between them.

So Tara, with some difficulty, put all other thoughts out of her head and concentrated on work. When the phone rang mid-afternoon, she naturally assumed it was someone wanting an appointment.

'Tara,' Annie called, 'it's a Mrs Talbot for you.'

Tara immediately recognised the name. It was Daisy's headmistress. She hurried across the room and took the phone from Annie. 'Tara speaking. Nothing's wrong with — '

She didn't have chance to finish that question before the woman was babbling, 'It's Daisy. She's gone, disappeared, during afternoon break. We've looked everywhere. I can't understand it — how it could have happened. The gates are always kept locked; she couldn't have got out on her own. It's impossible.'

'I don't understand. Isn't someone out there with them?' Tara cried. 'A teacher, an assistant? It's a primary school, for God's sake. They should be.'

The headmistress broke in at that point. 'Usually there is someone, but Jenny — Ms Taylor — popped inside just for a minute, and — '

'Daisy had gone when she returned?' Tara groaned her despair, her terror, out loud. 'No, no, no — it couldn't have happened that quickly. Did no one see anything?'

But Mrs Talbot didn't seem to be listening. She was probably as panicked as Tara was. 'There's no one you know who could have collected her early, is there? Anyone, anyone at all? Her father, maybe?' Desperation had taken hold of her. It was there in her every word.

'No.' But was it possible that Ricky

had come back? Tara tried to think rationally. He wouldn't simply take her from school, though — would he? Not without letting her know. But all of a sudden, she wasn't entirely sure about that. Her brother could be very erratic, thoughtless, dangerously immature at times. Hence his sudden disappearance. Maybe he'd decided he wanted Daisy with him, wherever he was, and had returned to collect her? Oh God, if only she could believe that. Panic once again overtook her. This wasn't Ricky. Deep down, she knew that.

'I've rung the police,' Mrs Talbot was telling her, 'but if you could come — '

'I'll be there in a couple of minutes.'

'Please hurry. I can see the police have arrived. Tara,' the headmistress's voice broke, 'I think someone must have taken her — it's the only explanation.'

Tara wasted no time. She called to Annie, 'I have to go. It's Daisy. Something's happened to her.'

As she ran to her car, all she could think was that Gray had been right. She should have told the police all that was happening. How could she have been so stupid? Criminally so. She'd placed her niece in danger. The anonymous caller had actually told her he'd take something precious. He'd meant Daisy.

With a sob, she pulled her phone from her jacket pocket and rang Gray, but all she got was his answering service. She left a message, garbled it was true, but she was sure he'd understand what she was telling him. 'I'll be at Daisy's school. Mallow End Primary.'

In another couple of seconds, she was on her way there. Mrs Talbot and Daisy's class teacher were in the office with two plainclothes detectives, a man and a woman. Both teachers were weeping.

Tara burst in, her breath coming in huge, sobbing gasps. 'What's happening? Tell me — how the hell could she have disappeared? From a school playground?' She looked at the two detectives. 'What have you done — or are doing — to find my niece?'

It was the female who answered her. 'I'm DS Barrett, and this — ' She indicated the man. ' — is DI Jones. We've begun an immediate search, Ms Wyndham. Not just the local force, but neighbouring forces are also involved. An alert has gone out. We will find her — but, obviously, the more information you can provide the better. Now we've spoken to Daisy's friend, Melanie, and she told us that a man appeared at the school gates and told Daisy her daddy wanted to see her. He then lifted her over the gate, which, as it's only four feet high gate, was a relatively simple task.' She slanted a reproving glance at the headmistress, which only served to intensify the woman's weeping. 'He then proceeded to put her into a black car and drove away. Do you have any idea who that might have been?' She eyed Tara keenly, as if trying to see right inside her.

Tara didn't hesitate. All that mattered now was that Daisy was found — safe. She told them everything that had been happening: Ricky's disappearance, the phone calls, the anonymous letters, the black car outside the house, and finally the threat to take something precious of Ricky's. 'If I'd thought for one minute he meant Daisy . . . ' She broke into tears of anguish. 'How could I have been so stupid?' She turned to the headmistress and said accusingly, 'Why didn't you talk to Melanie straight away?'

But the police weren't interested in her angry words. 'You should have reported all of this, Ms Wyndham,' DI Jones told her.

'I-I know that now, but I was afraid that Ricky was in some sort of criminal trouble. I never dreamt . . . I'm so sorry.' Tears poured from her eyes. This wasn't the headmistress's fault; it was hers, all of it.

The door into the office slammed open and Gray stood there, a young teacher following him, desperately saying, 'I'm so sorry, Mrs Talbot, but he wouldn't be stopped.'

Gray ignored her, his gaze going

directly to Tara. 'H-he's t-taken Daisy!' she cried. 'And it's my fault. Oh, Gray.'

He strode to her and took her in his arms. 'It's going to be all right. I'm here. Sssh.' He then regarded the two detectives, his eyes dark and determined, and demanded, 'What's happening? What are you doing about this?'

It was the DI once again who responded. 'Every force in the county and beyond have been notified about the missing child. A search has been started. We need all the information you can give us. Everything. A description of Daisy, exactly what she's wearing, a photograph.'

The questions seemed to go on forever. Tara had a photo of Daisy in her handbag which luckily she'd thought to pick up as she rushed from the salon. She handed the photograph to DS Barrett.

'Right, I'll get this circulated to all forces. Please try not to worry too much, Ms Wyndham. We'll do everything we can to find her. Now, I suggest you return home, in case her father returns or the kidnapper contacts you.'

'Yes, of course. Gray — ?'

'I'm coming with you.'

And he did. They returned to discover another envelope on the doormat. Tara tore it open and pulled out the single sheet of paper.

WE'VE GOT DAISY. TELL RICKY IF HE DOESN'T RETURN OUR GOODS OR THE MONEY FOR THEM, YOU WILL NEVER SEE HER AGAIN.

'No, no, no,' Tara screamed, collapsing into Gray's arms.

He took the sheet of paper from her and at the same time, and with the hand that wasn't holding Tara, dialling the number DS Barrett had given him. Tara heard him talking as if through a fog as he repeated the words written on the paper. After which, she managed to drink the small brandy he gave her. Lord knew where he'd dug that out from.

'It should help with the shock,' he gently told her.

But it didn't. Tara suspected that nothing would, not until she had Daisy back with her again, safe and unharmed. All she could think was how frightened the little girl must be.

'Oh God, I must ring Lizzie. She'll go to the school expecting to pick Daisy up.'

'I'll do it,' Gray told her.

Once he'd done that, Tara's mobile phone rang. It was Annie. 'I can't speak to her,' Tara said, her voice shaking as she handed the phone to Gray.

Gray told Annie what had happened, and finally promised to call her the second they knew anything.

From then on, everything became a blur for Tara. More police came and went again, searching Daisy's room as well as the rest of the house, looking for Lord knew what. If they found anything to help them in their search, they didn't inform Tara or Gray. They simply left again as suddenly as they'd arrived. Tara and Gray had remained in the sitting room. Tara had already supplied them with Ricky's mobile number. They could maybe trace when and where it had been used, but she didn't hold out much hope. Despair engulfed her, swamping her in misery and anguish, as again and again she berated herself for not informing the police sooner.

'This is not your fault,' Gray repeatedly told her. But Tara was convinced it was. If she'd reported everything to the police as he and Bel had urged her to, then maybe Daisy's kidnapping could have been prevented.

However, her doubts as to whether the police would trace Ricky's phone and thereby discover his whereabouts proved misguided. Within a very few hours, they'd traced the very last time it had been used to Spain. The Costa Del Sol, in fact. That must have been before he'd turned it off, or lost it, the latter seeming the most likely. Because surely if he'd received her text messages and seen all the missed calls from her, he'd have responded? Not even Ricky could be callous enough to simply ignore her.

He would have guessed how worried she was about him.

A couple more phone calls by the police established the fact that he was indeed there and had been picked up by Spanish police a couple of days ago, slumped in the street, high on drugs and not a single euro on him. He also had no identification. He was now in police custody. Tara hadn't even known he had a passport.

'We'll get him brought back to the UK as soon as possible.' DS Barrett informed her. 'In the meantime, we'll try to find out who this person is who's taken Daisy. We'll soon have your niece back with you, Ms Wyndham. Please try not to worry.'

⋆　⋆　⋆

And somehow, they did just that.

It turned out that the man who'd been stalking Tara was a contact of Ricky's who'd regularly supplied him with drugs, both for his own use and for

265

sale on the street. Ricky would then pay him what he owed. But this time, it had been different. The amount of drugs he'd given Ricky would sell for several thousand pounds rather than hundreds, DI Jones told her, and clearly the temptation had been too great. Ricky had disappeared, along with the quantity of drugs, and so hadn't paid his supplier what he owed. What had happened to the money he would have received for selling them was a mystery. As were the whereabouts of his car. In fact, the Spanish police hadn't been able to get any sense out of Ricky other than what had led him to travel to Spain: the desire to get as far away as he could from the man who'd supplied the drugs, thereby keeping the money he'd stood to make for himself. They suspected he'd been robbed of most of the remaining drugs and what money he'd managed to make, and so had been left destitute with no means of returning home even if he'd wanted to. As for his phone, what had happened to that was also a mystery.

Ricky had, however, supplied the name of the kidnapper, one Drew Wilmot, who was well known to the UK police as a dealer. Given the subsequent publicity surrounding Daisy's abduction, he'd obviously undergone a change of heart and, in fear for his own well-being, had taken Daisy to the nearest police station and left her outside. He then went on the run.

When Tara finally saw her niece between the two detectives, she broke down. 'Daisy, darling,' she wept, holding the little girl close.

'Where's my daddy?' Daisy asked tearfully. 'That man told lies. He said he'd take me to him and he didn't.'

Fortunately Daisy seemed relatively unharmed by her experience, going into some detail about her kidnapping. 'He gave me sweets and he had toys for me. He was quite a nice man but he wasn't my daddy. Where is daddy, Auntie Tara?'

'He's being looked after for the

moment, sweetie. He's not been very well. But I'm sure you'll be able to see him soon.'

Ricky would be held in police custody upon his return to the UK. However, Gray, with the assistance of a solicitor that he knew of, was trying to get Ricky admitted to some sort of secure rehabilitation hospital or clinic where he would receive treatment for his addiction.

But Tara wasn't sure about Daisy seeing her father at this stage in the proceedings. If Ricky was really ill, as was likely, and mentally unstable, it would simply upset the little girl all over again. And she didn't need to endure that sort of ordeal.

Tara glanced nervously at Gray, who had been standing to one side as Tara and Daisy kissed and cuddled. Daisy glanced at Gray too. 'Will you look after me, Gray? Until Daddy comes home?'

'I most certainly will. In fact, if Auntie Tara agrees, I'd . . . ' He hesitated, as if unsure whether to go on.

' . . . like it if you both came and lived with me at my house. You'll be safe there, and looked after. I'll guarantee that.' He glanced at Tara, who was literally silenced by what he'd just suggested. 'Tara?'

'Well — um . . . '

'What I'm trying, so clumsily, to ask is — will you marry me? I know it's all a bit quick, but we can take our time planning it, and it will mean we can get used to — '

She didn't let him finish. 'Yes, yes,' she hastily agreed, 'I will.'

He grinned at her. Daisy clapped her hands and began to dance on the spot. 'Can Daddy come and live with us too?'

'Daisy . . . ' Tara began uncertainly. There was no guarantee that Ricky could be helped to end his addiction to drugs, or that he wouldn't be charged by the police with drug dealing, despite all that Gray was trying to do for him. 'You don't have to agree,' she softly told him.

'I know,' he replied equally quietly,

'but I'm sure with the right treatment, Ricky will have the best chance. Maybe this experience in Spain will convince him that the life he's been living isn't any good, not if he wants to keep Daisy. If that doesn't happen and he's charged, well . . . ' He shrugged. 'She's got us. We'll deal with all the rest as and when.'

'Are you sure? You'd be taking on a ready-made family.' She eyed him doubtfully. After all, they barely knew one another, despite their having made love.

'I have no doubt that everything will work out perfectly. I love you so much, I'm not letting you go. And I was rather hoping . . . ' He eyed her, an uncharacteristic hesitancy on display. ' . . . that we'd eventually start our own family as well. But that's all for the future. For now.' He went to the jacket that he'd thrown over the back of a chair and reached into a pocket. He brought out a small box. 'And to make it absolutely clear that I will never change my mind, will you wear this?' He opened it and showed her a magnificent solitaire diamond ring. 'I'm hoping I've guessed the right size.'

Tara held out her left hand, and he slipped the ring on. Of course, it was a perfect fit.

'Oh,' she breathed, 'it's beautiful. When did you get this?'

'A couple of days ago — just in case.'

'Let me see, Auntie Tara,' Daisy cried.

Tara held out her hand.

'Oh, it's beautiful.' She looked up at Gray. 'So does this mean you'll be my uncle?'

'It certainly does. Is that okay with you?'

'Yes, yes,' she shrieked, clapping her hands in utter joy. 'We'll be so happy, all of us.'

Tara looked at Gray. He smiled, his eyes filled with a love there was no mistaking. Yes, she mused, they were indeed going to be so happy.

She mouthed 'I love you' at him.

He held out his arms. She walked into them.

'Me too,' Daisy cried. Gray leant down and picked her up, before putting his arm around Tara once more. And so, the three of them stood, together — for always, Tara was positive.

We do hope that you have enjoyed reading this large print book.

Did you know that all of our titles are available for purchase?

We publish a wide range of high quality large print books including:
Romances, Mysteries, Classics
General Fiction
Non Fiction and Westerns

Special interest titles available in large print are:
The Little Oxford Dictionary
Music Book, Song Book
Hymn Book, Service Book

Also available from us courtesy of Oxford University Press:
Young Readers' Dictionary
(large print edition)
Young Readers' Thesaurus
(large print edition)

For further information or a free brochure, please contact us at:
Ulverscroft Large Print Books Ltd.,
The Green, Bradgate Road, Anstey,
Leicester, LE7 7FU, England.
Tel: (00 44) **0116 236 4325**
Fax: (00 44) **0116 234 0205**

Other titles in the
Linford Romance Library:

THE LOCKET OF
LOGAN HALL

Christina Garbutt

Newly widowed Emily believes she will never love again. Working as an assistant in flirtatious Cameron's antiques shop, she finds a romantic keepsake in an old writing desk. Emily and Cameron set off on a hunt for the original owner, and the discoveries they make on the way change both of them forever. But Emily doesn't realise that Cameron is slowly falling in love with her. Is his love doomed to be unrequited, or will Emily see what's right in front of her — before it's too late?